ARTEMIS CITY
SHUFFLE

A NANSHE CHRONICLES PREQUEL
JESSIE KWAK

First edition October 2021

Cover art by MiblArt

Edited by Kyra Freestar

www.jessiekwak.com

Raj

L ife is an ocean. When the seas are stormy, it's
instinctive to fear the water, but on a clear blue day,
you let your guard down. You turn your back to the ocean.
You don't notice the sneaker wave until it has swept in
and tumbled you out to sea in a tangle of limbs and shattered dreams.

If you're sharp — or, more likely, lucky — you'll ride
the wave when it comes. If you're slow, you could spend
the rest of your life puzzling over the aftermath.

Raj Demetriou glances up from Ruby's message to
check the time on the interplanetary arrivals board, barely
takes note that the *Delanatia* — the pleasure cruiser from
the planet Indira he is waiting for — docked in Artemis
City's passenger terminal fifty-two minutes ago. Ruby's
words have hit him with that hollow one-two punch of
surprise and inevitability.

Never turn your back on the ocean.

He probes delicately at the feeling; around him, the
buzz of the crowd waiting in the arrivals terminal is a slow
crescendo of impatience, the edges of the sound going

wavy in the polished cement-and-ceramic cavern. An announcement in three languages blares muddy out of the intercom. Someone laughs at her companion's joke. One of the twin toddlers playing restlessly on the floor beside Raj jostles him, and her father shoots Raj an apologetic grimace. Raj gives him an automatically reassuring smile, but his mind is light-years from this increasingly restless crowd.

MAYBE YOU'VE A DEATH WISH, Ruby wrote. BUT MY BROTHER NEEDS ME TO COME BACK HOME ALIVE AFTER EVERY JOB. AFTER HOW BAD THAT LAST GIG WENT SIDEWAYS, I CAN ONLY ASSUME YOU'RE TRYING TO GET YOURSELF KILLED — AND I'M NOT GOING TO BE THERE WHEN IT HAPPENS. GET YOUR SHIT TOGETHER, I MEAN THAT AS YOUR FRIEND.

Ruby writes like she talks, which makes it easy to read the message in her voice: a velvety alto that always seems on the verge of laughing, pitched sharper with that touch of exasperation she usually reserves for her little brother. Or Raj, when he's pissed her off.

And he has, because Ruby's got one of those genius hacker's minds full of meticulously filed details, and she's taken the time to get comprehensive with her grievances.

He glances up from the laundry list of ways he's failed to adequately prep for jobs and checks the time on the arrivals board again — fifty-seven minutes have now passed since the *Delanatia* docked — his mind still stuck on "death wish."

Ruby thinks he has a death wish, which is fine. She can think whatever she wants; Artemis is a free planet and she's never been one to keep her thoughts to herself. But the fact that Raj's business partner — *former* business partner? — took the time to meticulously enumerate *why* she thinks he's a failure almost makes him believe her last line:

I WILL NEVER WORK WITH YOU AGAIN.

Three years ago, Raj's world imploded and he found himself tumbling breathless and wild in one of fate's sneaker waves. If things had been a heartbeat different he would be dead; instead, he washed up in Durga's Belt clutching fistfuls of aftermath. Now, watching the numbers on the interplanetary arrivals board blink higher and higher, Raj can't decide if this is one of those moments, too, or simply another piece of shrapnel from when his life detonated three years ago.

Doesn't matter which, though. His business part-ner — and the one friend he thought he had left on this rock — is done with him.

Not done, *done,* he tells himself, revising Ruby's note in his mind and smoothing down the sharp edges of the words. She'd think differently if she could see him now — not chasing some harebrained gig off the bounty boards for shady underworld bosses but taking a respectable, boring security job.

The arrivals board announces one hour since the *Delanatia* landed, and Raj straightens, cracks his neck. One hour is plenty of time for the first of the pleasure cruiser's thousands of passengers to be done winding their way through customs. Any minute now, those triple glass doors will slide open and the *Delanatia*'s passengers will begin flooding the waiting area.

The crowd around him knows it, too. The waiting area crackles with anticipation and frustrated boredom. A baby has started working itself up to a wail somewhere out of sight, and whatever game the twins next to Raj are playing has expanded to include the space around his feet — their father winces apology at Raj again and bribes them back with candy that smells of sticky faux mango. "Daddy will be here any minute," he tells them.

It's easy to see who's waiting for family and who's waiting for clients.

Raj falls into the second category: practical gray suit, clean black shoes, black hair glossed back into a short ponytail at the nape of his neck. He sorts through the other bored suits in his mind: taxi driver, driver, tour guide. Most are yawning into their fists or sitting with that rapid-blink, unfocused look that says they're playing a game on their lens.

No other bodyguards, though, at least not in the area he's staked out to wait. He can't decide if he's surprised or not. On the one hand, Artemis City is one of the safest places in Durga's Belt. It's the executive capital of the Pearls, the chain of dwarf planets that sits like a glittering buckle amid the rest of the asteroids in Durga's Belt. It doesn't have the rough-and-tumble reputation of the Pearls' constitutional capital, Ironfall, though neither of them deserve that reputation at all. Hiring a bodyguard here is a waste of money.

On the other hand, Raj has been made to understand that his client is some sort of deep-pocketed inner-planet socialite on vacation to visit her grandson. And Raj grew up on Indira among people just like her, the sort who travel via pleasure cruise if they ever deign to leave their home planet. The upper crust of Indira think anywhere in Durga's Belt is filled with space pirates and murderers and crime. He tries to imagine telling his aunts and uncles — his *mother* — that Artemis City is perfectly safe to visit without hiring extra security. They wouldn't travel here in a million lifetimes.

It's what makes Durga's Belt the perfect place for Raj to hide — unless, of course, he burns all his bridges with the few people he trusts out here.

Raj will do his part to make whatever heiress or society matron who's hired him comfortable. But until those triple doors open, he's on his own time. He swipes open a message to Ruby.

I'M SORRY. I KNOW THINGS TOOK A BAD TURN WITH THE MUGISHA JOB, BUT I'LL MAKE IT UP TO YOU ON THE NEXT ONE — I PROMISE. SAY HI TO YOUR BROTHER FOR ME AND LET'S TALK SOON.

He stares down at the message a long time before sending. Maybe she's right about him leaping into jobs without doing his due diligence. Maybe he hasn't found his footing since he washed up here with all his safety nets in tatters. Doesn't mean he's trying to get himself killed on *purpose*.

A fresh gust of excitement stirs the crowd around him, and Raj hits Send. One of the twins drives a sharp toddler elbow into Raj's thigh — the dad doesn't notice this time, he's straightened with the rest of the crowd to search for his partner. Raj gives Little Needle Elbows a silly scowl that makes the kid giggle, then holds up the blank green sign he's been instructed to bring in lieu of being told his client's name. An hour and seven minutes since the *Delanatia* docked, and the triple doors slide open, letting through the first trickle of passengers.

Raj jumps as his comm chimes.

He gives the incoming crowd a quick scan, then thumbs the comm open discreetly, hoping for a follow-up from Ruby. His disappointment is mitigated by rising intrigue when he sees the message is from Vash, instead.

A video message, as usual, which he doesn't understand, since Vash is blind. The angle is off — also as usual. Maybe she just doesn't realize the camera on her comm is on, maybe she just doesn't care. Her long gray hair is tied in a bun, her fingernails stained with engine grease. The subject of the message is New job?

Raj slips his comm back into his pocket without playing the message and goes back to scanning the crowd. Jobs for Vash and Gracie don't pay well, but they come with a perk: getting to sit and visit with the couple afterwards. They may be clients, but they make him feel at home — something worth clinging to in a place where he's making fewer and fewer friends every day.

He'd love to go pick up whatever weird trinket Vash wants and then spend a week on their quirky, junk-studded asteroid listening to Gracie lecture about art history while Vash tries to talk him into trying out whatever weird new tech she's working on — an exploding shield prototype is what she gave him most recently; he hasn't been desperate enough to use it.

He'd love that. But he can't afford it after how badly that last job went. Maybe he'll have enough of a cushion once this security gig is over.

And maybe he shouldn't respond. If Ruby's out, it's only a matter of time before Vash and Gracie throw in the towel on him, too.

"Ty Morgan?"

The trickle through the doors has become a flood; Raj straightens with a bright smile at the boxy grandmother who barked out his alias du jour like an order. As though he'd flipped a switch, his mind is focused and present — putting aside whatever's come before and whatever's coming next, just like was drilled into him at Mar-Alif

Officer's Academy, well back before his personal sneaker wave.

"Yes, ma'am," Raj says.

"Glad to see you're punctual. I hate to wait." The old woman is grandmother-shaped but Raj wouldn't describe her as soft. Her steel-gray hair is curled tight against her scalp like armor, face well-lined and coppery, mouth firm-set and turned down. She's wearing a smart skirt suit only slightly rumpled with travel, and jewelry that's expensive but understated; she probably was told to leave the flashy stuff at home. Raj scents her perfume over the constant undercurrent of filtered air and faint antiseptics. Subtle florals with a hint of spice.

"It's nice to meet you, Mx. . . ."

"Marta," she says brusquely. "And this is Jirayu, my driver."

Raj hadn't realized she wasn't alone; a lanky middle-aged man in an unobtrusive suit is skulking behind her with a neat cap of black hair and a faint smile on his thin lips that doesn't make him look happy. Jirayu gives Raj an automatic nod then goes back to scanning the room like a restless panther.

Who has the money to not just hire — but *travel with* — a private driver?

"I'm looking forward to our trip today," says Marta, and Raj pushes the thought away. Doesn't matter who she is back home. Here, she's his responsibility.

"Well, where to, ma'am?"

"I have a few places in mind," she says. Sparks of humor light up her dark eyes. "Are you armed?"

Raj blinks at the question. He's got a pistol in a shoulder holster, a knife in his boot, but he never uses either if he doesn't need to. If it hadn't been in the contract, he would have left the gun at home.

"Yes, ma'am?"

"Good. Let's start with some shopping in the Bell."

Marta marches away without waiting for him; Raj falls in beside Jirayu, matching his casual-yet-businesslike stride to the other man's prowl.

If Ruby could see him now, he thinks, she'd reconsider. Just a normal security job, taking someone's grandma shopping in the Bell.

Perfectly, utterly normal.

2

Lasadi

The mark is Logan Niñerola, and he doesn't seem to suspect his day is about to get very, very bad.

Lasadi Cazinho pretends to peruse a stand of tourist trinkets — holocards blazing with Artemis City tourist hotspots, plush children's stuffies of the planet Artemis with stitched-on eyes and wobbly arms, gaudy necklaces with each of the Pearls dangling from flaking faux-gold chains — and watches him out of the corner of her eye.

Niñerola's an elderly man dressed like a banker, with a narrow blue tie and white hair shorn close to his pink scalp. His wealth is in the understated rings on his knuckles, the gold in his pale earlobes, the subtle hints of gentech therapy around his jaws and eyes.

He may be dressed like a banker, but something sharp under the civilian trappings pings subtly at Lasadi's attention. Having spent the last three years around gangsters like Nico Garnet, she's become good at spotting the wolves among the lambs; Niñerola stands out like a neon sign in the crowd of tourists who've piled into Qāf Sector this afternoon.

The sector is busier than normal. A goliath pleasure cruiser from Indira docked a few hours back, apparently, and the tourists have come to shop Artemis City's most famous retail platforms.

Lasadi tunes them out; they're not important.

"What's our window?" she murmurs.

"Fifteen minutes," Jay says in her ear. "A quick cup of coffee and news, then he heads to collect from the shops on his route. You could set your watch by his schedule."

"Ballsy, getting into a routine like that."

"Don't get cocky, Las. You don't get to his age and rank in this business without being quick on the draw."

"I never get cocky."

Jay snorts laughter in response.

She loves this part of a gig. The golden, dawning moment where all potential outcomes spool ahead of you in a chain of fast, complicated equations. You've made your plans, you've checked your systems, and you're as prepared as you're gonna get. Once the engine fires and the ship comes to life around you, all that stands between success and failure are your wits and skill and guts — and your partner.

And when you have a partner like Jay Kamiya, you can get through anything.

Lasadi knows his voice better than she knows her own. He's got a touch more of a Coruscan lilt than she has, always edged with a smile like he just heard a good joke and can't wait to share it. No matter how many scrapes they've gotten into over the years — whether fighting together for the CLA or in these strange wasteland years since — she can count on one hand the times she's heard panic in Jay's voice.

Wasteland years, indeed, whispers a ghost in the back

of her mind. From a fighter in the Coruscan Liberation Army to Nico Garnet's errand girl.

She shakes the voice out of her head. The cause she used to believe in — a free Corusca — died three years ago in a battle that should have killed her. Maybe she's working for a criminal while she gets her feet back under her, but she's got a plan. She won't be Nico's errand girl for long.

"Las, you good?"

Jay's not even here — he's at a safehouse a few sectors away — and he can still read her like an open book. Anyone else, she'd hate how well he knew her. With Jay, it's reassuring.

"Just getting the feel." Lasadi swipes credits at the tourist stand to pay for her map, then moves closer to the shopping arcade to study Niñerola in the reflection of the store window.

This is probably the safest place to be in Artemis City, whether you're a citizen, a tourist, or — like Niñerola — the highest ranking of Kasey Aherne's captains. The city bores deep into the core of Artemis, the largest of the dwarf planets studding Durga's Belt. The surface levels are all docks and shipbuilding yards; the deep core levels are orderly layers of housing, office complexes, headquarters of industry. But the Bell is the main commercial hub. One hundred stories of open well, with buildings layering the walls and a latticework of bridges and suspended pedestrian plazas spiderwebbing through the center.

Pedestrian plazas like this one. Niñerola's here for a coffee at Campeche, an open-air stand set between a tour company offering day trips to the other Pearls and a shopping arcade featuring a creepily realistic display of strutting headless mannequins.

The sector's packed with people today. Living in close quarters never used to bother Lasadi — from tripping over her siblings to the crowded barracks of the CLA, overcrowding is a perk of living on a moon base like Corusca where real estate is tight. But she's grown comfortable with solitude these days. Besides the doctors who put her back together and Jay's occasional chucks on the shoulder, no one has touched her for three years; the crush of bodies around her makes her skin crawl.

Niñerola collects his steaming coffee cup from Campeche's pickup window, then sits at a nearby table and swipes open the business news.

"Always the same table," Lasadi says. "You were right."

"I'm always right."

"I thought you said don't get cocky."

"*You* don't get cocky," Jay says with a laugh. "I'm on fire."

"Whatever, big shot. What else do I need to know?"

"The thing about Niñerola," Jay says. "He considers himself quite the upright member of the business crowd. Attending charity events, investing in new business ventures outside of Aherne's organization, stuff like that."

"Explains why he'd risk security for a cup of Campeche's," Lasadi answers. "It's all about the image." She scans the tables around him. "No way he's here alone, though."

"He's not," Jay says. "Those tanks at the table next to him?"

"I see them." The first has bushy eyebrows drawn into a permanently perplexed scowl, his shoulders straining at the seams of his nice suit jacket; the second is a looker and he knows it. His shirt is undone a few too many buttons, eyeliner laid thick to make those artificially green eyes pop, hair swept up in a rock star wave. "His bodyguards?"

"Yep. They're quicker than they look, so stay smart."

"Always do."

"You know, if we'd hired a hacker like I said, you wouldn't be trying to pick the pocket of one of the most dangerous men in Artemis City. Just saying."

"This way's more fun."

"Is it?"

Lasadi can almost hear Jay's long-suffering glance at the ceiling — *Old ones give me strength.* "We can talk about it later," she says.

Though if everything turns out well on this job, maybe Jay won't bring it up again. Two is the perfect number for a team.

"Hey," Jay cuts in. "Look a little to the left."

Lasadi frowns, searching the reflection for whatever has caught Jay's attention. She can't see Niñerola anymore at this angle, and it's not until her gaze shifts past her own reflection in the glass — a phantom with pale skin and blond braid — that she realizes what Jay's trying to get a better look at through her lens.

A glittery purple purse set with holographic rhinestones.

"How much is that?" Jay asks.

"Jay. We're in the middle of a job, not shopping for your girlfriend."

"I need a peace offering before we head back to Ironfall."

"She kicking you out?" It's a joke; Chiara's head over heels for Jay.

"Keeps dropping hints we're gone too much."

"Then you might need more than a purse, my friend."

Lasadi laughs, but the conversation is prodding an uncomfortable old ache. There's no reason for it — Jay's happy, Lasadi likes Chiara, and despite the years they've spent as partners, Lasadi's never thought of Jay as more than a comrade and friend.

Just, Lasadi can't help but think one day she's going to turn around and Jay will be bouncing Chiara's baby on his knee and she'll be . . .

She'll be happy for her friends. That's what she'll be.

"Chiara'd like it though, right?"

The purse is awful, but Lasadi has to admit that the frilly woman Jay's fallen for would love the gaudy thing. She forces the tension out of her shoulders. "I'm not sure about the purple," she says. "There's a green one here that'd be killer with that leather jacket she likes to wear." She clocks the price tag and whistles. "And it'll cost you half your cut. If that's not a good peace offering, I don't know what is."

She straightens, checks on Niñerola; he's still reading his business news. "Now that I'm done shopping for you, can I get back to work?"

"All systems go," Jay says. "You are relieved from shopping duties."

"Thank the olds."

Las steps away from the shopping arcade window, feeling her way back to that golden moment. Around her, the pedestrian plaza fades into a general ruckus of voices with the airy acoustics of the Bell: competing music from storefronts, a baby crying, a pedestrian yelling at a moto-taxi driver. In the center of it all, Niñerola scans the news, oblivious.

Anticipation is electric on the back of her tongue.

Lasadi activates the tourist map she bought at the

nearby stand and begins threading her way through the tables, turning the map upside down as though trying to make sense of the honeycombed latticework of holograms shooting from the mini projector in her palm. Niñerola's muscle notice her first and watch her warily — Bushy Eyebrows glaring and Rockstar Hairdo giving her ass an appreciative once-over. Niñerola himself only spares her a glance when she sits at the empty table beside him.

"Excuse me," she calls across the aisle between their tables. "Do you know how to get to Hotel Telio?"

He frowns up from his news feeds. "The what?"

"Here." She stands back up and angles the map towards his face, the hologram honeycombs so close they dazzle him; he blinks and leans back in his chair. "I think it's in Dāl Sector."

Niñerola's jaw tightens, but he's still playing at respectable businessman, he'll help the distressed tourist. He squints at where she's pointing. "Dāl is here in blue."

"Where?" Lasadi tilts the map and he reaches out to steady her hand, leaving his comm resting on the table.

"Here."

Lasadi's fingers brush against his comm. "Oh, the green section?"

Niñerola lets out an exasperated puff of breath. "The blue. Here, if you look — "

A shot cuts him off, the crack of a bullet slicing through the rest of the noise and leaving a high ring like breaking crystal in its absence.

Niñerola roars to his feet before Lasadi even realizes what has happened, screaming in rage and reaching for his own gun, blood streaming from his shoulder. The second shot catches him through the throat and he falls back onto the table — body covering his comm. A spray of blood spatters his chest.

Lasadi dives below the table, though she's probably in no danger now. The shots came from above, at a distance — a sniper targeting Niñerola alone. She gives it a few breaths in the stunned silence that follows, and when no more shots come, she gets back to her feet. It's not hard to play the panicked tourist — her mouth is bitter with the spike of adrenaline, heartbeat pounding in her ears. She reaches for Niñerola like she's trying to check his pulse, steadying herself with one hand on the table where she last saw his comm.

Her hand closes around the shattered glass screen. *Dammit all.*

Someone grabs her arm — one of the muscle-bound young men at the table beside Niñerola's, the one with the bushy eyebrows.

"Who the hell are you?" Eyebrows asks. Behind him, Rockstar has a pistol in his hand and is yelling wild epithets in the direction the sniper shot from.

Lasadi stares at Niñerola, then Eyebrows, in feigned terror. "Oh my god! Is he dead? I was just trying to get directions."

"You were distracting him." The grip on her arm tightens, Eyebrows deepening his glare. "Deliberately."

"I don't know what you're talking about! Ow!"

And as always, Jay is there, his voice calm in her ear. "Okay, Las. In three, two — "

At "one," the table under Niñerola crumples with a hollow thud, an explosive in the table's single central column weakening the metal. The muscle-bound tank holding Lasadi leaps back in surprise and she whirls out of his grip, sprinting toward the transport lanes ringing the plaza with shouts of "Stop her!" at her heels.

"Always sits at the same table," Jay says with satisfaction.

"Good one," Lasadi says. She leaps over another table, scattering cups behind her in a sharp haze of good coffee and terrified screams, searching for her exit. And she grins.

Oh, yeah.

One of the Bell's ubiquitous mototaxis is idling at the curb, all neon pink and banana yellow. Its driver is leaning against the taxi stand, trying to chat up a fare — Las dives past him, behind the controls, kicking the engine into gear and tearing away into the stream of traffic.

"Tell me the sniper was part of our plan?" she asks.

"Negative," Jay says. "I'd say we just tore up the instruction manual on this one."

3

Raj

The flash of neon pink and yellow catches Raj's attention before he can consciously understand what it is; his body moves before he realizes he's reacting.

"Ma'am!"

Raj catches Marta's arm just as one of the Bell's nuisance mototaxis comes careening around the corner in the wrong direction, a streak of eye-bending hues and equally colorful language from the driver yelling for them to watch where they're going.

"Watch it yourself," Raj yells back at her, saving the choicer phrases he would have used for a time he's not with a client.

Marta yelps in surprise, teetering on the curb a moment with gnarled fingers clawed into Raj's forearm. When she catches her balance, she pats a hand over the tight coils of her steel-gray hair, eyes wide.

Marta's first stop is Qāf Sector, a trio of interconnected platforms suspended around Level 10 of the Bell. From here, Raj can't make out the glass dome that tops the Bell, or the busy docks beyond where the enormous pleasure cruiser *Delanatia* and her hundreds of smaller sister ships flow in and out of the mouth of Artemis City.

The dome is almost ninety stories up, obscured from view both by distance and the lattice of bridges and platforms that span the Bell's circumference. The floor of the Bell is only about ten levels below them; beyond it, Artemis City continues to bore into the planet another few hundred levels. Most tourists never leave the Bell, and Raj doesn't blame them. He grew up with Indira's vast horizons and atmosphere — he'll never be used to the warren of cramped passages those who grew up in Durga's Belt seem comfortable with.

But the Bell is strange in its own way — it's like being inside a neon bottle, the tangle of sloping walkways and bridges and lift lines and spiraling trams spinning you around in the glitter. The light never changes, giving the disorienting illusion of whatever time of day you want it to be. It thrums with activity at any hour. Kids in bewildering fashion heading out to — or home from — clubs mix with smartly dressed office workers and belt drifters in greasy coveralls, each on their own schedule.

Different pockets of space within the Bell have their different vibes. In Qāf Sector, tourists and locals alike are here to see and be seen, sipping coffee and cocktails in open-air cafes, pressing their noses against the glass windows of the shopping arcades, strolling the walkways arm in arm and admiring the glitter of the Bell arching around them.

And dodging the mototaxis that zip passengers around the sector. Getting hit by a mototaxi is practically a rite of passage for visitors to Artemis City, but Raj isn't going to let it happen to Marta on his watch.

"You all right, ma'am?" he asks.

"I am, thank you." She releases his arm. "There are more of those than the last time I was in Artemis City."

"How long ago was that, ma'am?"

The question comes out before Raj realizes he's asked it; he was too busy glaring after the mototaxi to remember most people who hire bodyguards are looking for a slice of muscle to stand in the background, not a friend to chat with. But Marta doesn't seem to mind.

"A decade, maybe," she answers. "How long have you lived in the Pearls?"

"A few years." The third anniversary of his arrival in exile was seventeen days ago, but who's counting?

"From Arquelle?"

Raj smiles ruefully. "I try not to advertise that."

"You Arquellians have a particular way of drawing out your vowels."

Marta seems satisfied at guessing his home country rather than suspicious that he's Arquellian, so he'll count that a win. He hasn't been able to decipher her accent; it doesn't sound like any Indiran country he's aware of, but it's not quite the Pearls, either.

"And after you're done here?" she says.

"I'm sorry?"

"When you're done in Artemis City," Marta clarifies. She gives him a sidelong look. "Or have you moved here for good? A young man like you must have plans."

In his mind's eye he can imagine Ruby waiting for his response, too. Arms crossed, hip cocked, one perfect eyebrow arched: *Well, then?*

He gives Marta an easy smile. "Not sure yet. Was Jirayu bringing the sedan around here?"

"Yes," says Marta. "He'll meet us here. Come, there's one more store I want to visit."

Marta accepts the change of subject without pressing, but Raj doesn't relax. He tells himself the near miss with the mototaxi has him on edge, but the truth is her simple question's stirred up too many ghosts.

At one point, every step of his life had been planned out. Graduate with honors, just like his father had. Attend the Arquellian navy officer's school, Mar-Alif. Get his commission, take a command post, earn his stripes in glorious battle, become an admiral.

Just like his father had.

Back then, he'd wanted nothing more than the chance to make his own plans. But even when he did dare dream, he hadn't breathed those dreams to a single soul; he twists the cittern string fashioned into a bracelet on his wrist. It's the only flotsam remaining from his past life.

And now?

Security drones swoop past with lights glaring, and Raj glances up, grateful for the distraction. There's a commotion on the far end of the pedestrian plaza where a handful of tables cluster near a coffee stand. Marta watches the drones go, curiously.

"The security drones are quick to respond anytime there's an incident," Raj assures her. He doesn't need her getting worried about local crime. "Probably someone twisting an ankle. I'm sure it's nothing."

"I hope so," Marta says. She turns her attention to the nearby shopping arcade, where headless mannequins are pretending to walk the fashion floor with the latest styles. "Shall we?"

Raj follows her, with one last glance back across the plaza. Along with the drones, a pair of security guards have arrived to manage the gathering crowd. Through the shifting legs of onlookers, he can make out a lone figure sprawled on the ground but not what took them down. A medical incident, maybe; Raj hopes things will be cleared up by the time Marta's done with her shopping.

He's never been in this particular boutique before — these days he couldn't afford a necktie from the display, never mind one of the suits — but Marta walks in like she owns the place. Exactly as his mother would have done: shoulders back, head high, an indulgent smile at the shop-keeper who comes scurrying over.

Marta's entrance says she's got money, and it's not just the shopkeeper who notices. A young man with shaggy blue-dyed bangs follows them in, far enough behind to make it seem like a coincidence, but Raj has noticed him following them for a few minutes now. Either he's shop-ping for his own granny or he's got an eye on Marta's purse. Raj scans the store, keeping an eye on Bangs; even if the way he's dressed didn't put him out of place here, the sharpness around his eyes would give him away.

When Marta heads to the dressing room with the shopping attendant in tow, Raj pulls out his comm and pretends to check his messages. Bangs edges closer to the dressing room as though examining the row of shoes; as soon as the shopping attendant comes back out, Bangs slips in.

He makes a beeline towards Marta's cubicle.

Bangs has one hand on the door, the other pulling a knife out of his pocket when Raj clamps a hand over his mouth from behind. The kid yelps hot breath against Raj's palm, heart rate rabbiting and arms windmilling — the knife whooshes past Raj's ear, too close for comfort. Raj slaps a tranquility patch against the side of Bangs's neck.

Bangs goes limp. Raj catches him, wrestles him as

quietly as possible into the cubicle next to Marta's, then trusses the kid's wrists and ankles and leaves him lying on the floor before letting himself out.

"I'd like to try this in the blue."

Now it's Raj's turn for an adrenaline spike; he whirls to Marta's cubicle to find her door cracked open, her outstretched hand holding out a green jacket with glittering buttons and bell sleeves. Raj takes it from her without a word — the shopping attendant hasn't been saying much anyway — and steps out of the dressing room. The attendant is staring at him, wide-eyed.

"She'd like to try this in the blue," Raj says, handing the man the jacket. "And you have a thief in Cubicle 3. Please wait to call the police until we're on our way — I don't want to disturb the lady, and the thief isn't going anywhere for a bit."

"Yes, sir."

Unlike Raj's mother, Marta is a quick shopper who knows what she wants and makes firm decisions. She chooses the blue jacket, a smart black jumpsuit, and a brightly patterned scarf. The attendant's eyes widen when she presses her finger to his pad to pay; whether she's left him a tip or he recognizes her name, Raj can't say. The man just bows to them both as they leave.

The commotion on the far side of the plaza has indeed been cleared up by the time they leave the boutique, and now Jirayu's back, lanky frame tipped against Marta's elegant sedan with ankles and arms crossed, eyes half-closed.

Where the hell were you while I was thwarting a pickpocket? Raj thinks irritably, but this guy's the driver. Raj is the bodyguard.

Jirayu takes the shopping bags from Marta and hands

her a recyclable cup from the roof; Raj catches the whiff of good coffee from the steam.

"Successful shopping trip, ma'am?" Jirayu says.

"Very much so," Marta says, then turns to Raj. "Have you been to the Zoraya Gallery?"

"I've been past, never inside."

"I hear wonderful things about the current exhibit. Is it close?"

"It's just a few levels away."

"Good!" Marta smiles brightly and settles herself in the back seat of the sedan. Jirayu closes Marta's door behind her and meets Raj's gaze; something glints deep in the dark pools of the other man's eyes, but before Raj can read the emotion it's gone.

"I hope you like art," is all Jirayu says.

4

Lasadi

"You're having too much fun," Jay says in her ear.

Lasadi grins and drops the mototaxi through a vertical gap in the traffic at an intersection, then revs the engine to zip into the flow of traffic a split second before the thrusters shut out and the wheels hit the roadway.

"I am not, I'm working."

"Sure," says Jay. "I've seen the way you eye those things. You've been looking for an excuse to steal one for years."

"You're just jealous you're not getting to drive." Lasadi swerves around a parked delivery drone, dodging oncoming traffic with a whoop.

"I'm just glad I'm not in the passenger seat."

"If you didn't like flying with me you could have asked for a transfer."

"And leave you in the hands of an inferior mechanic? Anyway, you're a fine pilot. Just don't know what you call *this*."

"Escaping." Lasadi shoots the mototaxi through an alleyway and screeches to a halt beside a closed loading dock. She can't go much farther; mototaxis are coded not to be able to leave their sector.

And not that Jay's *entirely* right, but she has been curious about taking one for a spin. Most have a narrow bench that can seat two behind the driver, with a luggage area in the back that makes a great target for thieves. The mototaxi handled far better than she was expecting, though it's top-heavy and she got it up on two wheels more than once when careening around a corner. She guns the engine experimentally, then cranks the handlebars and releases the brake, testing its limits in a tight circle.

"Las."

"Okay, now I'm playing."

She hits the hand brakes, and the mototaxi's third wheel thuds back to the ground. This mototaxi has a union sticker in the window, which means it'll have a working tracker and the owner will be able to recover it quick — they may already be on their way here. By the time they get here, though, Lasadi will be long gone. She's already walking away from the mototaxi, fast enough to put some distance between her and the stolen vehicle, casual enough that she won't attract attention.

She's ended up near the lowest levels of the Bell, where shipments that come in from the docks at the top of the Bell get staged for distribution throughout the city below. There's a wholesalers market around the corner, if she remembers right, distributors selling cheap or damaged goods to locals straight out of the shipping crate. She heads that way, walking with purpose; even though she doesn't yet know where she's going, she knows she can get easy transport from the market.

"What the hell was that back with Niñerola?" she asks. "You find anything out while I was driving?"

"You mean while you were joyriding? Yeah. I found out that this job is over."

"Not a chance. Nico sent us here because he knows we deliver." She presses against the side of the wall as a woman in a forklift suit trundles by with a pallet of liquid oxygen. "Question is, were we set up? Or was that a coincidence."

"Doesn't matter which — our mark is dead. We've been compromised."

"I think it was a coincidence," Lasadi says, ignoring him. "Niñerola was obviously killed by a sniper, so it's not like someone was trying to set me up. I just caused the perfect distraction for the real killer. Has it hit the security feeds yet?"

"Yeah. Stand by." She doesn't have to see Jay's face to guess he's got that stitch of concentration between his dark brows, he's scrubbing a hand over his jaw. "They're looking for a lone sniper. No mention of an accomplice."

"How about the mototaxi?"

"Ah, yes, your vehicular theft." Another pause. "Not reported to security, so the driver probably went straight to the union. Personally, I'd rather get caught by security."

"I'm on my way out."

"How good a look did Niñerola's tank get at your face?"

Lasadi pictures Eyebrows grabbing her arm, tries to remember how much he would have seen of her. "Not that good," she says. "And it doesn't matter, because Aherne's captains each run their own separate crews, so he won't be around the others."

"I don't like it. Something's up."

"Then figure out what it is. Who's next on the list?"

"Stand by."

They'd picked Niñerola as the easiest of Kasey Aherne's captains to get close to, but all three of them will have the same access codes to his townhouse on their comms. With Niñerola out of commission, it's just a matter of getting close to the next most likely candidate to pickpocket.

Sure, Jay's right in that if they'd hired a hacker, they could head straight to the townhouse and override the security from there. But this is such a small work-around — or it would have been, if Niñerola hadn't gotten himself shot. Either way, they'll need those codes if they're going to bypass Aherne's security and get to the safe in his office, where he's keeping an unspecified object he stole from Lasadi's boss.

No, not boss. Client, maybe. The label doesn't matter, though, because she's only a few more jobs' worth of credits shy of buying the *Nanshe*. Then she'll be able to put the word *former* in front of her uncomfortable business relationship with Nico Garnet, and she and Jay can finally head out on their own.

Nico may be a mobster, but he supported Corusca's freedom from the Indiran Alliance. That alone doesn't make him a good man — she's been betrayed by people she trusted in the CLA before — but she'd be dead right now if his mercenaries hadn't scraped her out of her crashed and burning ship three years ago.

Her fingers brush the ridge of scar tissue in the hollow of her abdomen and she forces them back down at her side, shaking off the memory of scorched flesh and the taste of blood, the ship shuddering into pieces around her and Jay screaming her name in her ear.

She may not like Nico, but he's been fair to work for. And he sent her here to do a job, not get lost in memory.

"Jay? What have you got for me."

"JD Tirrand is up next," Jay says. "I'll send the details your way — I'm working on getting eyes on him."

Las slips into a doorway, props a shoulder in the frame while she reads the info Jay sent about the second of Aherne's captains. Tirrand is the youngest of the three, the flashy, hot-tempered enforcer to Niñerola's classy businessman vibe. In the still Jay sent, Tirrand's eyeing the camera like he's considering taking a crowbar to it.

"Tirrand's with family today," Jay says. "Visiting his mom at home."

Lasadi's comm pings with a location: a luxe pod complex a few levels away from the shopping plaza where Niñerola was just killed. "What's the plan?"

"Once you're in place, I'll bluff a call to get him out for a meeting in the lobby. You'll have to be quick — the instant he realizes the call's fake, he'll be on his guard."

"Can you get me a better view on the place?"

"Sending. The optimal spot to wait is going to be at the corner of — hold on."

Jay swears under his breath on the other end of the line. Down the corridor, someone's yelling frantic directions to a delivery driver; the shriek of metal on metal and a stream of curse words says the driver didn't listen.

"Jay?"

"I'm hearing some chatter on the police frequency about a second murder."

"Besides Niñerola?"

"Yeah. They — fuck. They're talking about Tirrand. Someone strangled him just around the corner from his mom's place."

"Are you serious?" A chill creeps down Lasadi's spine. "What the hell is going on?"

"Come back to the safehouse, Las. Whatever's happening, we don't need to be a part of it."

"We need those access codes."

"Someone's killing Aherne's captains. Either they're after the third one, too, or she'll be running back to safety."

Lasadi pushes off of the doorframe and heads for the bank of pneumatic lifts that whisk passengers throughout the Bell. "Or she's the one doing the killing."

"That's a big assumption."

"You've been reading up on her. She's a climber. This is totally in character."

That sharp intake of breath, he doesn't disagree. "Then she'll be vigilant."

"We need those codes, Jay."

"Nico will understand. You couldn't have planned for this."

Nico probably *will* understand. But he won't pay them for a job not finished, and she's not about to stop when she's so close to saving what she needs to buy the *Nanshe* from him.

Lasadi slams her palm on the button to close the lift door.

"We *need* those codes," she says again. "Point me in a direction."

5

Raj

One summer when Raj was nine, he'd been swimming at a resort town on Arquelle's Emerald Coast when his foot got caught in a discarded fishing net. The adults were at a pre-dinner cocktail reception at the club, the nanny'd had one eye on the gaggle of navy officers' brats and the other on the svelte lifeguard, and Raj had slipped away.

At first he'd panicked, struggling to kick his foot free, but every thrash in the water made the net bite in harder, ducking him under the waves, which were a touch deeper with every swell. He tried to call for help, choking on lungfuls of water, throat raw with salt and bile — it had probably only been a minute but it felt like hours by the time a local fisherman spotted him and dove in to cut him out.

Raj had sworn the fisherman to secrecy and borne his father's tongue-lashing for being late to dinner in silence. Even at that age he knew better than to ruin their illusion of a perfect family having a perfect day.

Now Raj tilts his head, studying the eerily violent

tangle of glass and wire in front of him that's supposed to be art. Good art evokes feelings, he supposes; this piece evokes the claustrophobia of being trapped and drowning, flailing for life. Not something he'd want hanging in his dining room.

The exhibit at the Zoraya Gallery is called *Trivial Influences*, by an artist listed as a famed zero-G sculptor from one of the Bixian settlements. The darkened hall is filled with a series of strange, wispy sculptures that are meant to illustrate "the profound loneliness and enhanced humanity of life in the deep black." An over-sized hologram of ice giant Bixia Yuanjin spins slowly against the far wall.

Raj finds the sculptures unsettling, and not just because the gallery's gloom makes it difficult to keep an eye out for danger. Each sculpture is suspended in the darkness, illuminated by strategic spotlights and pinpoint lasers in shifting hues. Some of them seem almost humanoid, limbs twining together in a way that could be dancing — or violence. He can't tell if they're meant to be erotic.

He turns away from the tangled sculpture he's been studying — it's titled *Nihility Limits III* — to find that Marta has finished her first round and is back to study one of the smaller sculptures, an amorphous blob with spiraling crystal fins. Raj scans the gallery as he joins her; from what he can tell, the other people here are as confused as he is by this exhibit and trying to hide it.

The plaque on this sculpture — *Vascular Spheres VII* — claims to represent a heart expanding and contracting in the vacuum of space, the heating and cooling of the crystal while the sculpture cured pumping ink through tiny passages to create spiderwebbed veins of gold and black that seem to bunch and expand as the sculpture slowly spins.

"Do you have children?" Marta asks without looking away from the sculpture.

"Gods, no." Raj glances from her back to the plaque. There's no mention he's supposed to be thinking of his progeny while viewing the statue.

The corner of Marta's lip twitches in a smile; Raj's first instinct was right. She's looking for a bodyguard who can hold his own in a conversation, not a silent hunk of muscle.

"A bit of unsolicited advice, for if you ever decide to," she says. "Raising a child is like these sculptures. You can shape the material according to your plan, but you can't control the end result. You have to be at peace with that."

Raj laughs. "Try telling my father that."

"It's a lesson my son never learned, and it killed him in the end."

Raj can't help the sharp glance; little old tourist Marta is still studying the statue, but in this moment she looks more youthful, fiercer. The finer lines on her copper skin are smoothed by the eerie light, her eyes spark like flint.

"I'm sorry for your loss, ma'am."

That breaks the illusion of youth: when Marta meets his gaze, he catches a flash of deep weariness. "Another bit of unsolicited advice," she says. "You're better off leaving the family business to someone you can fire rather than someone who shares your blood."

Raj frowns at her. "You're . . . here about your family business?"

"I'm here to see my grandson. He's not well." And the conversation's over; Marta's shoulders square and she lifts a hand to the gallery owner, who's been keeping herself nearby. She scented the aura of money around Marta the minute they walked in.

"I think I'll take this one," Marta calls.

Raj trails Marta and the gallery owner through the surreal gauntlet of suspended translucent statues to a thankfully more well-lit area of the gallery, then takes a position outside the gallery owner's door.

Marta's comment about her grandson bothers him, but he can't parse whether it's what she said or because this job has roused what his father called his melancholy streak. That penchant to indulge in a moody current of memory and flights of fancy, plucking out shining, ephemeral flashes of inspiration to spin into a poem or a song. Raj can picture his father's dark look around the Zoraya Gallery, he can hear exactly what he'd say about the display: "Some people have too much time on their hands, and didn't get enough discipline as children."

Raj had gotten plenty of discipline as a child, and he'd never been allowed much time on his hands. Every minute of every day was planned out, every step of the rest of his life. It had felt like being caught in that net, with every minor act of rebellion dragging him deeper until he finally bucked against his father so hard that he ended up here — basically as good as dead. Nothing worth working for but another night's sleep in a shitty pod.

He can picture Ruby rolling her eyes: *Oh, go off, will you?*

Okay, so maybe he hadn't vetted their last job as well as he should have — maybe he's gotten a bit sloppy. Maybe he's gotten so trapped in the net that he's stopped looking for a way out.

He should have known taking a job for Sara

Mugisha — reigning empress of Artemis City's party scene and designer drug trade — would come with a twist. She needed some intel, she'd said, a quick freelance job to find some dirt on someone she wanted leverage over. She was willing to pay double what Raj would normally charge, and he'd talked Ruby out of her initial objections.

Only problem? The target was Kasey Aherne. Where Mugisha is the empress of the party scene, Aherne's empire is solidly blue collar — or at least, it always had been. Turns out these days he fancies himself a refined gentleman, with a refined taste in drugs. And he owes Mugisha an obscene amount of money.

Raj doesn't care what Mugisha's plans with Aherne are — only thing he knows for certain is he took an unnecessary chance and triggered Aherne's safeguards, and Aherne will be a deadly enemy if Ruby hasn't covered their tracks well enough.

Oh. And that Mugisha doesn't pay for compromised intel.

Something nags at Raj's attention, and he blinks his thoughts back into the present. Scans again, trying to figure out what his subconscious was trying to point out to him.

There. The custodian.

A man in Zoraya Gallery coveralls is pushing a cleaning cart towards the offices, but he stepped right past a discarded flyer without stooping to pick it up. Could be he's on his way to his break and can't be bothered. Or could be something's up — especially with the furtive way the man is scoping out the gallery's guests.

Raj detaches himself from the wall with a quick backwards glance at Marta; she and the gallery owner are still negotiating a price. He pretends to be bored, making a round of the art while he waits, and out of the corner of his eye he catches the glance the custodian flicks his way before making a beeline towards the office.

Raj approaches him silently from behind, tapping the man's shoulder as he reaches for something on his cart.

The custodian jumps.

"Excuse me," Raj says. "I got something on my jacket. Can I bother you for a cloth?"

"What?"

"A cloth. I got some hot sauce on my jacket, I think." Raj leans past the man as though reaching for one of the folded cleaning cloths. At this angle, he can see exactly what the custodian was reaching for. A silenced pistol.

Raj twists sharply, swinging his elbow back to crack across the custodian's jaw. The man stumbles into the wall with a groan and Raj grabs him by the collar, throwing him through an open door and into an empty office.

A nearby woman in a blue suit — an office type on her lunch break — glances their way in surprise. Raj shoots her a bright smile. "We've got an issue with the lighting," he says, and closes the door behind him.

The office appears to be a smaller version of the gallery owner's: a pair of elegant chairs in front of a glossy black desk, tasteful art on the walls. Raj grimaces. There's not a lot of room to maneuver, way too many delicates around to make a mess of.

It'll have to do.

Raj slides a finger up a control panel marked Music and the gentle percussion of the ambient music in the gallery kicks up — hopefully enough to mask the noise they're about to make in here.

The custodian lunges across the room at Raj; Raj

ducks the man's punch, dancing back out of reach with shoulders loose. Feints a left hook in order to get closer to the statue in the corner — it looks like cast copper and falls like it, too, crashing against the custodian as he tries to scramble out of the way.

Raj grabs him by the shoulders and throws him against the desk, but the custodian recovers quickly. He catches himself against the edge of the desk and ducks Raj's swing, coming up under Raj's arm to slug him in the gut. Raj pivots with the punch to lessen the blow, then grabs the custodian in a headlock. A pair of solid punches to the man's kidney drop him to his knees; Raj catches the man's neck in the crook of his elbow, squeezing until he slumps forward.

Raj checks the custodian's pulse — still strong — then rolls him over, rifling quickly through his pockets for any form of identification. The overalls are printed with a name, T. Tovs, but they're probably stolen. And given the backup weaponry this guy is carrying, he didn't just get a wild hare to shoot up a gallery today. He's a professional, and he was either going for the gallery owner or for sweet little Marta.

The fight only lasted seconds, but that's too long to have been out of view if the custodian wasn't working alone.

Raj secures the custodian-slash-headhunter with a pair of disposable cuffs and lets himself back out of the office, straightening his jacket and smoothing stray strands of his shoulder-length hair back into its ponytail.

The woman in the blue suit gives him another glance, but it's more appreciation than suspicion. He winks at her; she blushes and goes back to studying the art.

Marta and the gallery owner are still in her office, and

no one seems to have noticed the fight, so Raj pulls out his comm.

His connection request to Ruby is rejected — not shunted into a voicemail queue, but flatly denied. He's about to try again when his comm chimes with an incoming message.

Don't call me.

Raj sighs. I need you to ID someone for me. I'm sorry. It's important.

Fuck you, Raj.

Raj takes a surreptitious picture of Marta, then collects every detail he knows on her and the listing from the job board. He sends it to Ruby.

I'll make it up to you.

He's waiting for a snarky reply — *I guess I'm bailing you out of trouble again, what would you do without me* — but his message to Ruby remains unread. Raj slips his comm back into his pocket just as Marta steps out of the gallery owner's office. She gives him a quick once-over, gaze touching on the abandoned custodian's cart behind him.

"Is everything all right, Mr. Morgan?" she asks.

"It's wonderful," he says. "Is everything all right with you, Marta?"

Her smile quirks to the side. "Splendid."

She thanks the gallery owner and heads to the front door. Raj follows after giving the gallery owner a quick rundown on the incapacitated headhunter situation in her spare office. His comm remains silent.

Jirayu is waiting at the curb, lounging against the sedan. He straightens when he sees Marta and holds open the door; he's sporting a new pair of black leather gloves.

"Are you hungry?" she asks them both. "I'm simply famished."

"Food sounds good, ma'am," Raj says. The double punch of adrenaline between the pickpocket at the boutique and the custodian-slash-assassin at the art gallery has sparked his appetite.

Jirayu gives them both a smile — the first real one Raj has seen. "I know just the place," he says. Is it Raj's imagination, or has the driver's mood been lifting with each stop they've made? Jirayu and Marta share a look that's muddied and opaque with secrets.

Something's wrong with this job, Raj decides. Something's very, very wrong.

He spares a glance at his comm before slipping into the passenger seat beside Jirayu, but his message to Ruby remains unread.

6

Lasadi

The Bon Mirage is a classic stop for tourists and Artemis City locals alike. The restaurant's decor went out of fashion long enough ago for it to have come back around with an aura of charmingly nostalgic kitsch, and during peak hours there's often a line out the door. Lasadi has never understood why. The food is passable at best, the drinks watered down, the crowds irritating, the servers harried.

The hour is a bit late for lunch, but the restaurant is still packed when Lasadi walks up to the front door. A young man — tawny skin, dark ponytail, exceptionally well-fitting suit — is holding the door for a woman who could be his grandmother; he nods politely for Lasadi to follow the old woman through, then gives her a professional once-over for threat assessment. Not the old lady's grandson, apparently — her assistant or bodyguard? He seems to find Las harmless, so she ignores him, too.

The scent of fried garlic and basil and steaming rice hits her as soon as she walks into the lobby. A specials board announces a variety of simulated fish dishes.

"I'm meeting a friend," Lasadi calls to the host, waving enthusiastically to a woman sitting alone at the bar and getting a confused look in return. The host barely glances at Lasadi before turning his attention back to the old woman.

She's been told the Bon Mirage is meant to mimic an Arquellian beach resort — something about the pressed bamboo paneling and plastic floral tablecloths, maybe. Lasadi has no idea if the Bon Mirage is hitting the mark.

The bar area is separated from the restaurant by a giant hologram of a fish tank, and while the rest of the original decor may be fraying and chipping around the edges, no expense has been spared on this illusion. It casts a blue glow over the scene, punctuated by brightly colored fish and gently wafting greenery. A ghostly ray the size of a table flaps pale wings to spin in a lazy circle; a purple-and-white-striped eel pokes its head out of a hole to examine Lasadi before darting across the bottom of the "tank." Lasadi pretends to admire the fish, but her attention is on the guests seated in the restaurant beyond.

"You see her?" Las murmurs. A school of tiny bronze fish flicker past inches from her eye.

"To your right," Jay says after a moment. "Middle of the room."

Lasadi spots her now. Kasey Aherne's third captain, Lora Kirr, is a tall woman with blue-black skin, wearing a classic green tunic dress embroidered with gold swirls. She finishes giving her order to the waiter, then swipes up a screen on her comm with an annoyed glance at the door.

"She looks relaxed," Lasadi says. "Must not have heard about Niñerola and Tirrand yet."

"It's not on the news. But Aherne's people would have told her."

"Maybe someone's keeping it from her."

"Or you're right and she ordered the assassinations. I don't like this, Las."

Lasadi doesn't either. She can't decide if it's better or worse for Kirr to be ordering the assassinations. Either way, someone's making a massive play for power in the Aherne organization right as she and Jay are supposed to be breaking in to retrieve Nico's goods.

That could be disastrous. Or it could be just the distraction they need.

She wouldn't lose face if she stepped back from this job now. Hell, Nico might even recommend it if she checked in with him. But stopping now means taking one more job for Nico still — and it's not just about money to buy the *Nanshe*. Lasadi's been able to justify this arrangement to herself — and Jay — so far, but working for Nico Garnet isn't what either of them signed up for. Jay hasn't said it out loud, but he's been dropping hints that he's about to walk away from Nico whether Lasadi's with him or not.

"Let me get her comm, then we can make a decision from there," she says. "Anything else I need to know?"

Jay sighs. "She's waiting for one of her lieutenants. But I've engineered a little delay for them. You've got at most maybe five minutes before they arrive."

"I won't need it."

The waiter has returned to Kirr's table — or the manager, perhaps. A lanky, thin-lipped man with a cap of black hair is trading her empty glass for a new cocktail. "Compliments of the house," he tells her. Kirr barely glances up from her comm; she's taken a drink even before he walks away. Apparently she likes to start her evenings early.

Lasadi turns away from the rainbow schools of fish and heads towards the restaurant by way of the employee entrance to the bar, swiping a busser's apron and towel off a hook and grabbing an empty tray when the bartender isn't looking. She takes her time getting to Kirr's table, gathering a few empty glasses along the way, but no one gives her a second glance. Let alone Kirr, who's absorbed completely, comm in one hand, cocktail in the other.

Lasadi waits until Kirr is mid-sip before she stumbles, spilling the water glass in her hand all over Kirr's lap.

Kirr jumps up, swiping at her dress with a shriek. Las sets down her tray of dirty dishes on Kirr's table and tries to towel the other woman off. "Get away from me, you clumsy idiot," Kirr snarls, snatching the towel out of Lasadi's hands and daubing at the silk with a vicious curse.

Lasadi holds up her hands; she'd slipped Kirr's comm into her own pocket the instant Kirr traded it out for the towel. "Sorry, ma'am. Just trying to help."

"You have no idea who I am," Kirr snarls, but the sharp edges of her words are blurred. Maybe she's had more than the two drinks, or maybe the Bon Mirage mixes their cocktails stronger than Lasadi remembers. Kirr blinks at Lasadi like she's having trouble making her out. "You . . ."

"I'll get you another towel," Lasadi says. She bends to pick up her tray of dirty dishes once more; Kirr's fingers claw into her hand.

Kirr's eyes are wild, bloodshot with rising panic. "You — "

"Ma'am?" Lasadi breaks the hold, stepping back as Kirr begins to choke, flecks of foam on her lips. Kirr's hand flies to her throat. "I'll go get my manager."

But whatever is happening to Kirr is progressing so

fast that Lasadi wouldn't have had a chance to go for help even if she were the real busser. Blood trickles from Kirr's nose as she collapses back in her seat, shaking hand knocking the rest of her cocktail over. Glass shatters, red liqueur blooming over the flowered tablecloth.

The cocktail.

Compliments of the house, delivered by a lanky man in a suit who most definitely was not the Bon Mirage's manager.

Lasadi snatches her hand off the table before the liquid can reach her. In front of her, Lora Kirr takes one final, shuddering breath before her eyes flutter closed.

A horrible hush falls over the restaurant, and Lasadi's been standing in shock too long. She drops her tray and bolts, elbowing past a waiter and sending him lurching into a table — she briefly registers him colliding with the old woman and her bodyguard. Behind her, someone screams, "She just killed that woman!"

Lasadi dodges past the host stand and pushes her way through the waitlist crowd, her heart pounding in her ears.

7

Raj

Either Marta's seeking out trouble or she attracts it; it's not Raj's job to figure out which. It is his job to keep her safe from the surprising amount of trouble today is throwing their way.

His nerves are taut and ready, after the earlier incidents, and Raj is on his feet the instant the waiter crashes into their table. He has the waiter in a headlock and on his knees before Marta has even moved; her eyes go wide with surprise.

"Easy!" The waiter's yell comes out strangled, hoarse, but Raj pats him down anyway before releasing his hold. He's clean, as Raj expected — he wasn't there to attack Marta, one of the other staff simply knocked into him when she sprinted out the door. But between the pickpocket in the boutique and the custodian in the gallery, Raj has decided to be suspicious of everyone today.

"Are you all right?" he asks Marta.

Her lips purse in annoyance. "Something spilled on my blouse."

Raj hands her a napkin and she daubs delicately at

her waist, apparently unconcerned by either Raj's scuffle with the waiter or the scene that just played out a few tables away.

A woman has been murdered. Raj catches a glimpse of green silk, a dark-skinned arm flung out over the floral tablecloth, liquor or blood mingling with spilled water. And her face . . . *Oh, shit.*

The murdered woman is Lora Kirr.

A month ago Raj wouldn't have been able to pick Kirr out of a crowd, but after spending some time surveilling Kasey Aherne — her boss — he's gotten to know her face pretty well. He doesn't know enough about the Artemis City underground to know if she's got enemies of her own, but after that surveillance job he did for Sara Mugisha, he knows Aherne's in Mugisha's sights.

That job went wrong, and this job with Marta's going off, as well. But no matter what game sweet old lady Marta is playing, it's not safe to spend time in restaurants where members of Aherne's organization are getting assassinated.

"Ma'am."

Marta drops the napkin on the table and picks up a sweet roll, looks up at him with innocent eyes. "Yes?"

"We should probably try another restaurant. This one doesn't seem particularly . . . safe."

Marta waves an unconcerned hand, then pops a piece of sweet roll in her mouth. "Let me rest my tired feet a moment more. Then we can go."

"I know it's not usually in a bodyguard's job description to argue with the client," he says. "But I really must insist — get down!"

Something glints on the other side of the holographic fish tank. It could have been the flash of silver scales but for the red spark of a laser sight in the corner of Raj's vision.

Raj dives for Marta.

The sniper's bullet tears into the cushioned back of Marta's chair, splintering bamboo and sending a spray of foam and gel boiling out of the gash. Raj tumbles to the ground with Marta in his arms as another bullet strikes lower, tearing through the table and lodging in the floor an inch from Marta's elbow. A third shot sounds but Raj doesn't see it land.

He waits for a fourth shot to punch through the shattered glass chorus of screams — to punch through *him* — but nothing comes.

"Are you all right, ma'am?" Raj asks. He'd cushioned most of their fall — and he'll feel it tomorrow — but for now adrenaline is keeping any minor aches and pains at bay.

Marta's arm is flung over her head like it'll protect her from a bullet; when she lowers it, the sweet little tourist mask is completely gone. She doesn't look scared. She looks furious.

"Get him!" she snarls. Raj pushes himself up to a crouch in time to see a man with a rifle slung over his back sprinting past the host stand. Raj's pistol is in his hand before he knows it, he fires twice the second the assassin is clear of the host.

The assassin stumbles with a grunt, but doesn't stop running for the door.

"Go!" Marta orders.

Sniper normally means working alone, which means Marta is probably safe to be left behind. But this isn't the same assassin that killed Lora Kirr, which means there are two killers in the Bon Mirage. Maybe killer number one was the busser who ran out earlier, or the busser was a decoy for the real killer.

Either way, though, Marta has given him a direct order. Pure, cold rage fills her eyes and Raj pities anyone who decides to mess with the old lady right now.

Raj charges after the man with the rifle, vaulting the low wall that divides the restaurant from the lobby, noting the spray of blood on the doorframe with satisfaction. "Which way?" he yells at a bystander, who gapes at him and doesn't answer.

A scream from around the corner; Raj sprints towards the sound, scattering the gathering crowd of rubber-necked onlookers as he goes.

And skids to a stop.

Jirayu is waiting beside Marta's parked sedan, as usual. Only this time he's got the assassin on the ground, one knee pressed into the small of the man's back. The assassin is bleeding from the bullet holes Raj put in his thigh and shoulder.

Raj shoves his pistol back in its holster before the security drones can buzz in.

"Thanks, man," Raj says to Jirayu, who gives him a distracted nod and pulls a pair of disposable cuffs from inside his jacket, trussing the assassin's hands behind him. Strange thing for a driver to carry, but Raj appreciates that Marta and Jirayu are done pretending this is a normal gig by this point.

"She hurt?" Jirayu asks.

"She's fine," Raj answers. "I'll go get her."

"I'm right here, young man." Raj turns to find Marta pushing her way through the gathering crowd, purse held aloft in front of her like the prow of an icebreaker. She stops with her sensible heels inches from the assassin's skull, folds her arms and glares down her nose at him. "Well?"

"It looks like he was working alone, ma'am." Jirayu gets to his feet, one dress boot still grinding into the assassin's lower back; the assassin yowls in pain. "I apologize for letting him get so close."

"It's fine," Marta says. "That's why we hired backup."

"You're sure he was working alone?" Raj asks Jirayu. "Another woman was killed in there, and it wasn't by him."

The corner of Jirayu's mouth twitches into a smile. "I'm sure," he says simply, and that buzzing cacophony of what-ifs on the edges of Raj's mind resolves into a single, clear note. Marta's not traveling with her own personal driver, she's traveling with an assassin of her own. Jirayu killed Lora Kirr — and who knows what else he's been up to while Marta and Raj have been out shopping and gazing at art.

Marta lifts an eyebrow at Raj as an invitation to commentary, but he keeps his mouth shut. He may not know who Marta is, but he understands how things work around here. Someone's got it out for her, which means her trouble is his trouble unless he decides to forfeit a payday.

He can hear what Ruby'd say: *Now here's a great time to walk away, isn't it. Just say, "Hey man, this gig is a bit more than I signed up for," and get the hell out of there.*

But her voice is just in his imagination. Raj's comm has remained silent — Ruby hasn't even bothered to read the message he sent her asking her to look into Marta's identity. Not that her help would have made much difference at this stage. Raj was in too deep before he ever sent that message.

Jirayu gives the man at his feet a shove with the pointed toe of his dress boot. "What would you like to do with him, ma'am?"

"Ask him a few questions." She glances from the assassin to Raj, then turns her back, seemingly satisfied with whatever she sees in Raj's face. "Bring him."

Marta steps past the man on the ground without waiting to see if Raj will follow her order.

Every job has this moment, when the tide turns and what you thought was solid washes out from under your feet. It may not be the big, life-shattering sneaker wave, but it can be just as deadly if you're not paying attention. And it comes with a choice.

Raj can ride it out, see where it takes him and if the opportunity's worth pursuing. Or he can step out of the surf and head back to the life he knows. The one with the empty bank account, shitty rental sleeping pod, and no one who will answer his calls.

Jirayu's waiting for his move, eyes bright as obsidian. Raj can't quite decide if Marta's "driver" would let him walk away even if he wanted to.

Whatever game Marta is playing is dangerous. Marta herself is clearly trouble. But Raj is intrigued despite it all, and if even his business partner — sorry, *former* business partner — is refusing to read his messages, what does he have to lose?

Raj bends down and hauls the assassin to his feet, marching him after Marta.

8

Lasadi

L asadi slams the door to the safehouse shut behind her and collapses back against it, panting for breath.

It's stifling in here — a hotel room barely one step up from a body locker, with a fold-down bed, a side table, and its own toilet. Jay's taken over most of the available space: duffel bag of electronics strewn over the bed, portable desk unrolled on the side table. He's in fraying work pants and a loud promo shirt for what looks like a Coruscan kafusa band, what with the daggers and skulls emblazoned across the chest. The sleeves are cut out to reveal well-toned pale brown arms. He looks up at her, blows a lock of shaggy black hair out of his eyes, and grins. A dimple tugs at one cheek.

"Nice work," Jay says. He swipes away the 3D map that had been hovering over the desk in a tangle of streets and passageways he'd had to lead Lasadi through. "That last jump was impressive."

"Wouldn't've had to jump if you'd sent me down a better alley."

"Faith, Las." But the dimple smooths. "You hurt?"

"I'm good."

A stitch appears between his brows, the desk light pooling in his dark eyes not quite hiding the worry. Irritation snaps through her, but she reins it in. She remembers a time when they'd fly back to base whooping at their near misses and marveling at their adventures. A time when they laughed off minor scrapes, when the possibility that one of them might not actually come back seemed absurd.

She knows exactly what broke that spell of naivete. Maybe if Jay had been the one to almost die in the Battle of Tannis, she'd be checking him for cracks after every mission.

She didn't die then, and she hasn't brushed close since — but for some reason, that edge of worry on his face is getting sharper each job rather than dulling with time.

"I'm fine, Jay," she says, letting annoyance seep through. She tugs Lora Kirr's comm out of her pocket and tosses it to him. "If I was hurt, could I have managed that wild chase you just led me on?"

"Sure, sure." His lips quirk to the side as he studies the comm. "Guess this is my bad luck, huh?"

"What, Lora Kirr getting poisoned?"

"No, you bringing her comm back with you. I'd hoped we struck out this time, too."

Lasadi laughs. "I guess we're stuck finishing this job after all."

"Maybe." Jay plugs the comm into his desk. "You get a look at whoever killed her?"

"I saw the guy who dropped the drink off — but the poison could have come from anywhere."

"They get a look at you?"

"I don't know." She'd changed her outfit up enough

that the casual observer might not have noticed that the tourist at Campeche and the busser at Bon Mirage were the same woman. But in her limited experience, assassins weren't casual observers. She scoots a tangle of cords out of the way so she can sit on the bed beside Jay, then starts pinning up her blond braid. She can wear a cap and a maintenance visor for this next part of the job.

"I scrubbed you out of the security footage, I think," Jay says. "So at least the Artemis City security won't be looking for you."

"You 'think'?"

"Hey, you're the one asking a ship's mechanic to do a hacker's job. I bought the login and code off an acquaintance and I can follow instructions. But who knows if it worked."

"I'm sure it's fine. And it's a good thing you're so multitalented — no one else would fit in this tiny safehouse."

His dark eyes flash to her, so brief she almost misses it. "Used to be you trusted a lot more people than just me." His tone is light, but there's more of that worry buried beneath it.

"Most of them are dead." And anyone from their CLA days that isn't? Lasadi no longer knows if she can trust them. All of which Jay knows, so Lasadi isn't sure why they keep circling this conversation.

"Dammit." Jay reaches for Lora Kirr's comm — the biometrics decryption program he was running simply returned a giant red error message. "Let me run that again."

"Don't make me take back what I said about you being talented."

Jay hits Start Decryption once more and leans

forward, forearms resting on knees as he watches the program run.

"I'm serious, Las. If we're going to do more jobs like this — whether for Nico or not — we can't keep doing it on our own."

"I'm serious, too. There's no one I trust like you."

"Maybe you should try talking to other people sometime." He says it light, like he's ribbing her, but the way the muscle moves over his jaw after belies his tone. Las wills the status bar below Kirr's comm to fill in faster, but it's taking its sweet time.

"I talk to people," she says after a minute.

"I mean besides marks." This time the look he flashes her holds. "Or Nico Garnet. I think — "

He breaks off to check the comm, but the decryption program is still running without error.

"You think what."

His lips purse.

"Jay. What is it?"

"I think I'm through working for Nico. So you may need to find someone else."

The words hit her like a kick to the sternum, if she hadn't been sitting down her knees might have buckled underneath her. She forces herself to breathe, eases the tension out of her jaw. Logically, she knows she has no hold on Jay — though somehow, she realizes, she truly thought it would always be the two of them. It was the two of them flying together for the CLA during the war. It's been the two of them these last three years working with Nico. And afterwards . . .

She hasn't allowed herself to imagine what comes afterwards, if she's honest. She's been telling herself it's a blank slate, a future she can write however she wants. But in reality it feels like a cliff she's about to step off.

She's not an idiot — she's noticed how different the lives she and Jay have been building from the ashes are. His includes his girlfriend. Chiara's family. His drinking buddies. His random contacts who keep trying to lure him away with job offers of their own. Lasadi's new life includes the only two things she can count on besides herself: Jay and the *Nanshe*.

The thought of losing either leaves her gut as empty as if her engine had stalled.

Jay's chin jerks up, though she doesn't think she let on how deep that missile hit. "For his jobs, anyway," he says. His voice holds a note of apology, but it's clear he's made his decision.

"That makes sense," she says, proud of how calm she sounds. "Not a problem." The screen flashes green — they've successfully accessed Kirr's comm — and Lasadi breathes a curse of relief. "Thank the olds."

"We're not done talking about this, Las."

"We are for now. What do you have for me?"

"One second," Jay says, scrolling through the comm. And his lips quirk into a smile. "Got it. Access codes to the security system in Aherne's complex."

"See? What do we need a hacker for." She winks and holds out her hand; Jay drops the comm in her palm.

"Okay," he says. "Obligatory last sanity check. Is continuing to break into Kasey Aherne's compound according to our plan a terrible idea? Or just a really bad idea?"

"A marginally bad idea," Lasadi says. "But I think" — she elbows Jay in the side as he tries to cut her off — "No, listen. Aherne's three captains were just killed. Which means his whole organization will be in disarray. Our original plan had us getting in without him noticing, and now he'll be more distracted than ever. It's perfect."

Jay scrubs a hand over his jaw.

"Am I wrong?"

"You're not wrong."

Lasadi grins. "Then let's go see Kasey Aherne."

9

Raj

In hindsight, it seems inevitable that Raj would find himself standing in the walk-in refrigerator of the Bon Mirage while Marta and her quote-unquote driver interrogate a screaming assassin hanging from a chain.

There'd been indications that something wasn't right, and he'd written them off. Take the fact that Marta traveled with her own personal driver to a planet with only a handful of private vehicles. Or the way Jirayu kept disappearing while Marta did her sightseeing. Consider the pickpocket that targeted her in the boutique and the custodian-slash-assassin at the Zoraya Gallery.

Any individual moment could have been brushed off — but put them all together and the implication is crystal clear: Raj is way in over his head once again.

The cold in the walk-in refrigerator should chill him to the bone, but he's too swept up in the moment to notice.

"Where is he holed up at?" Marta asks the prisoner again; she's back in grandmother mode, steel curls perfectly in place. Her hands are clasped behind her, fingers of one hand tapping against the back of the other in bored impatience.

The assassin grits out an answer through bloodied lips — it sounds like "Fuck you" — and Jirayu hits him once more with the electric barb. This time lasts longer than the previous ones, and when Jirayu finally lets him rest, the assassin's teeth rattle like a cabinet full of heirloom porcelain in an earthquake.

Marta takes a sharp breath, annoyed. "I sent my grandson a polite note requesting a meeting and he sent an assassin instead. Where. Is. He?"

Raj's job is technically to watch the door to the walk-in refrigerator — which is something Marta would have asked him to do from the outside if she didn't want him to see exactly what she's capable of. He gets the message: *You're involved now, too.*

He's just still not sure *what* he's involved with.

The assassin gave a solid swing at pretending he doesn't know who Marta is asking about before dissolving into insults, which means Raj is the only person in this tiny, frigid room who's clearly in the dark. He can hear Ruby's commentary: *I get that bodyguards are meant to keep their mouths shut, Raj. You couldn't have asked one question, only? Said, "Ah, your grandson's local, that's lovely. Anyone I should know? Some self with homicidal tendencies, maybe? No reason, just curious."*

Raj isn't fooling himself that he's not in this room by choice. Maybe Jirayu wouldn't've let him walk away from the shootout at the Bon Mirage, but Raj could've run. He could've shot first. Could've called security.

No, he's here because Ruby's right. He sensed this job jumping the rails, and instead of bailing like a sane person would do, he buckled in to see where the ride would take

him. The fact that it could've been straight over a cliff —
could still go that way — was part of the appeal.

Ruby called it a death wish, but it's not a wish — it's
an embrace of the inevitable. Three years ago a sneaker
wave shattered Raj's life, and for all intents and purposes
killed the person he'd been. He's just been waiting for
someone to put a final seal on the whole mess. And like a
drowning man tired of treading water, he's started cutting
away the people — Ruby and her little brother, Vash and
Gracie — who've been keeping him afloat.

At Jirayu's startled grunt, Raj turns his attention back
to the scene in front of him. The chattering of the assassin's teeth has gotten worse, and it's not just cold and electric shock. He's going into convulsions, foaming at the
mouth, eyes rolling back in his head.

"For heaven's sake," Marta says crossly. She steps
back, one hip bumping into a stack of boxes labeled TVP
Steak. "He took poison. Jirayu!"

Jirayu pulls a syringe out of his jacket pocket and
stabs it into the assassin's neck, but whatever magic he
was hoping to pull, it's too late. The assassin gives a final
shudder, then goes slack in his chains.

"Gods*dammit*." Marta exhales a sharp puff of breath
into the freezing air. "I suppose we'll have to do things the
hard way."

"I'm sorry, ma'am," Jirayu says, but Marta shakes her
head to dismiss the apology.

"I would have expected my grandson to hire sturdier
stock."

She heads for the exit and Raj pushes the door open
for her politely, aware of the absurdity of the formal
gesture; she's exiting a walk-in refrigerator where she just
murdered the man who'd tried to kill her. The chef

walking up to the refrigerator jumps when the door opens, the tray of puff pastries tilting in her hands.

"You may want to find another place to store that," Raj says to her. The chef's gaze slides past him in horror.

"Yes, my apologies," Marta says. "Please call security, we found a murderer."

Marta pats the chef kindly on the arm as she brushes past, then heads for the door, her sensible heels making soft scuffs against the self-cleaning mats on the kitchen floor. The chef nods frantically at Marta's back, her reply so faint Raj almost doesn't catch it.

She'd said, "Yes, Ms. Aherne."

Whatever warmth was starting to work back into Raj's body vanishes in a puff. His gaze snaps to Marta's face.

That square chin, the strong nose, broad brow always in a faint scowl — now that he's looking, he can see the resemblance. Marta tilts an eyebrow, watching this new piece of information work its way through Raj's brain.

Raj clears his throat. Pushes open the door to the street for Marta. "Ma'am? Your grandson is . . ."

"My grandson is Kasey Aherne," she says. "And he's running my business into the ground." She marches to the sedan, where Jirayu already has her door open, and pauses to study Raj. "You've more than earned your fee today, Mr. Morgan," she says to Raj. "But I will triple it if you're willing to stay by my side for the next few hours."

Raj blinks at her. She was already paying him well, and tripling that number would not only wipe out the debt he's got, it would give him enough to lie low for a while. Take a break from the constant treadmill and figure out what's next — not just stumble into the next job, but actually come up with a plan. Spend some time with

Gracie and Vash and Vash's weird experimental proto-types. Do some of that soul-searching Ruby seems to think he needs.

Not to mention that if he sees this through the right way, he could make himself a very powerful friend.

On the other hand . . .

"I know what happens to people who bet against Kasey Aherne and lose," Raj says.

Marta smiles. "I didn't get to be as old as I am by losing."

"What's your plan?"

"I have loyal followers who still work for Kasey. His three captains were not loyal, but I have people lined up to replace them."

The body on the ground in Qāf Sector. Jirayu's ever-increasing good mood. Lora Kirr wasn't the first of Kasey Aherne's captains Jirayu took care of. The other man flashes Raj a pleased grin.

Ah. Okay, then. Raj takes a breath.

"Aherne — your grandson — has been lying low in his townhouse for the last few weeks," Raj says. "The one in Bā. I'd guess he's still there now."

"Then we'll pay him a visit."

"Your plan is to knock on the door and hope he doesn't shoot first?"

"Would you come with me if I said yes?"

Why the hell not, says a dark voice in his mind, and he almost says it out loud. But maybe — just maybe — he's been riding this wave out to sea long enough. It's time to start swimming back to shore.

"That would be suicide," Raj says. "But, ma'am? If I may, I have another idea."

10

Lasadi

K asey Aherne makes his home in one of the expensive, nicer townhouse compounds in Bā Sector. The sector's centerpiece is a ten-story enclosed entertainment complex suspended in the center of the Bell, ringed with the glittering columns of townhouses and hotels. People who can afford to stay here pay a premium for a home or hotel room with actual windows — and there's actually something worth looking at, if you enjoy neon-smeared nightclubs and the fifty-meter-tall advertising holograms that swim around the entertainment complex.

Aherne's compound, called the Nightingale, features five columns of five townhouses each — every one advertised as having a view. From what Lasadi has turned up, most of the townhouses are luxury vacation rentals or pieds-à-terre. Only a few are continuously occupied — by people who value proximity to the nightlife over the relative privacy and security offered in other parts of Artemis City.

Which means it's perfect for their plan.

Lasadi slips the maintenance visor over her eyes when they enter, but the bored concierge doesn't even glance up at their faces when their keycards turn green. He's watching a tabloid stream, two people fighting cattily over the accusation that — as far as Lasadi can tell — they both wore the same outfit to an awards ceremony.

"Heya, this work order's wrong," Lasadi says, shoving a tablet in his face. She's dropped her normal Coruscan lilt into the rougher pattern of the Pearls. "It says the recyclers in Wing A but we's here for them last week, weren't we."

The concierge leans back in his chair, frowning at her tablet. "I don't remember that."

"Why would you? Place like this, stuff's breaking down all the time? It's not Wing A that's malfunctioning — we need to get in *E*."

"Wing E is restricted."

"Yeah? Well Wing E's about to be evacuated, and I'm getting paid whether or not you let me in, so that's your problem."

Beside her, Jay brushes a thumb over the open screen on his comm, activating the cheap AI he hired a hacker friend to overlay with a manager's anxious personality and train with specific details about the Nightingale's recycler system.

"I'll need to check," says the concierge. "I — just a second." An incoming connection request from Jay's Anxious AI Manager lights up the concierge's desk a split second later, pulsing yellow with emergency. The concierge swipes the call to his headset.

"Yessir?" The concierge flinches and touches a finger to his ear to turn down the volume. "Nossir? I hadn't heard anything about that, I . . ." He calls up a screen;

from this angle, Lasadi can't make out the details, but a "we have a critical problem" notification is flashing red and angry in the man's eyes as they widen.

Lasadi waves for his attention as he weathers the Anxious AI Manager's tirade. "Wing E," she says. "Give us a thumb."

The concierge presses his thumb into her tablet without taking his attention away from the call. Lasadi palms his master keycard while he's not looking and tosses Jay the tablet, calls thanks over her shoulder as they push the maintenance cart into the lobby.

It's meant to impress, and it does. The centerpiece of the lobby is a golden cage spanning floor to ceiling, surrounded by faux-marble benches. The cage is filled with towering plants, and songbirds flutter in the foliage. Maybe it's supposed to re-create the open forests of Indira? The vast swaths of green Lasadi grew up staring at overhead when the planet filled Corusca's sky?

"I can't decide if I like it," Jay says, staring at the enormous cage.

"It's creepy. What if they get out?"

"I watched a thriller vid once about a woman who was killed by hummingbirds," Jay says. "With enormous beaks. One went straight through her eye."

Lasadi shudders. "I don't think I ever need to go to Indira."

"I'd love to see the ocean."

"You've seen it."

Jay rolls his eyes at her. "I've seen it from Corusca. I'd love to see it standing on the shore."

"Then let's go."

Jay shoots her a look.

"We can go anywhere," says Lasadi. "Chiara — "

"Has no desire to leave Ironfall."

"We'll talk her into it. C'mon."

At the far end of the lobby, a complicated system of lifts fan people to each of the five wings. Lasadi pushes the bulky maintenance cart into the one labeled Wing E, and their new credentials deposit them a few minutes later in a smaller lobby.

The doors to each of the five townhouses are set in a semicircle around Wing E's lobby; each townhouse is a wedge of a semicircular column climbing the wall of the Bell. Aherne lives in Unit 4, which will be heavily guarded — but with most of the Nightingale's town-houses being vacation homes, the units to either side of Aherne's are currently empty. And Lasadi wasn't guessing when she commented to the concierge that stuff breaks down all the time at the Nightingale. It may have a glossy exterior, but the construction is slapdash and the wiring is all interconnected. It'll be easy enough to turn off Aherne's security from the control panel of another unit in Wing E, then slip from one balcony to the other.

Lasadi swipes the stolen keycard at Unit 5, then feeds the concierge's thumbprint into the biometrics to override the approvals. It blinks yellow twice — thinking — then turns green. She lets out a breath and grins at Jay.

And freezes.

The front door of Unit 4 — Aherne's unit — bursts open with a flux of activity, Aherne's men pouring out in a tumble of shouted orders. They're filling the small lobby, and even if Lasadi and Jay ran through the door of Unit 5 right now, they've already been noticed. One young tough checks his pistol, then frowns at Lasadi. Another pair have taken up position by the lifts, a mere meter away from where Jay and Las are standing. She risks them a glance, ducks her head.

Bushy eyebrows on the one, rock star hairdo on the other.

"What's wrong?" Jay hisses.

"Niñerola's guys," she whispers back. "From the plaza." Her arm still aches where Eyebrows grabbed her after Niñerola was shot. If he recognizes her now, it could be disastrous.

Before she can squeeze herself past the maintenance cart into Unit 5 and out of sight, Kasey Aherne himself comes storming out of his townhouse, buttoning his suit jacket over a shoulder holster. "I'm done playing games with that bitch Mugisha," he growls to the woman with thick black braids at his side. "She's through in this town."

"I've got the coordinates, sir," the woman with the braids says, but Aherne's not listening. His attention spears Lasadi like a shard of ice.

"What the fuck are you doing?" he asks.

"Waste recyclers," she says, her voice steady despite the adrenaline singing through her veins. "Don't know if you noticed, but it's about to become a whole problem."

"Fucking obviously," Aherne snarls. "And that unit's empty, isn't it. So get in here and do something about mine."

He steps out of the doorway, jabbing a scrawny finger for Lasadi and Jay to go into his townhouse. They share a look — Jay's expression says he likes this even less than the original plan — but to Lasadi's mind it's perfect. No worries about the alarm system between the units now, and Aherne's on his way out the door? Something's finally going according to plan.

Lasadi gives Aherne a lazy salute and drags her maintenance cart out of the doorway of Unit 5, aiming it at Aherne's townhouse instead. Jay clears his throat and follows.

Once the last of Aherne's crew flush out of the house behind him, Lasadi shoves the maintenance cart through the door. He'd mentioned Mugisha — he must mean Sara Mugisha. Is she the one sending headhunters after Aherne's captains? It doesn't quite make sense — not with what Lasadi knows about Mugisha's style — but she can puzzle through it later. Right now she's not here to step in the middle of a turf war. She's here to crack a safe and get the hell back to Ironfall. Lasadi's closing the door behind her when Aherne's voice stops her.

"Heya! You and you."

She keeps her shoulders relaxed, though she's anything but. She can feel Jay's readiness beside her, coiled and easy. "Yeah?" she calls.

But Aherne isn't pointing at her and Jay. He's pointing at someone outside her frame of vision. He jerks his thumb at the door. "Keep an eye on those assholes."

"Mugisha killed Niñerola," a voice complains. "We should be there to get revenge."

"She killed him because you failed at watching him," Aherne says, vicious. "Be glad I'm just giving you babysitting duty."

And the skin on the back of Lasadi's neck pricks, raw fear drying her tongue.

"You have to be kidding me," Jay mutters. Because of course the pair of men Aherne ordered back into his townhouse are Niñerola's men, Eyebrows and Rockstar. Of *course* they are.

"Go," Jay whispers. "I'll handle them."

He starts digging through the maintenance cart,

unloading vacuum attachments and bricks of sanitizer and the rest of their bounty of cleaning supplies in the entry while the two bruisers look on in confusion. He tosses a data stick to Rockstar, who fumbles as he catches it.

"Help me with that." Jay says.

Rockstar stares at the data stick like he's never seen one before. "This?"

Jay waves at the control panel near the front door. "Plug it in," he says with exasperation. "Before the whole system shuts down on us and we're up to our armpits in recycler backflow."

Rockstar makes tracks for the control panel; it takes him three tries to get the data stick in the right way, and the panel begins to glow green as the codes they cloned from Lora Kirr's comm grant Jay remote access to Aherne's security system.

Perfect.

Lasadi makes for the stairs — her target is two floors up — but a barked "Heya!" from Eyebrows freezes her with one foot on the first stair. He's pushed past Jay, his bushy brows drawn together, and Lasadi can see the flicker of recognition stirring his features. Her heart sinks before he can pull together the question.

"Don't I know you?"

11

Raj

R aj spins slowly in the center of the spacious warehouse, examining his work for the cracks.

For the resources he's got, it's not a half-bad plan.

He'd pulled in a favor with one of the dockworkers who'll still take his calls, securing them an out-of-the-way space where innocent bystanders won't get hurt if Marta's family feud comes to violence. Given the day's body count so far, it seemed smart to err on the side of caution.

The warehouse is prepped for a big shipment from a local hauler that got delayed by pirates deeper in Durga's Belt, so there's plenty of space to maneuver and no one will be looking to bother them. A few crates are staged for loading, a forklift suit slumps dormant near the door.

Marta's sitting behind a metal table, which Raj and Jirayu dragged below one of the spotlights in the middle of the space. It's suitably dramatic, of course, but it also serves to keep the attention on her and Raj rather than whatever Jirayu may be doing in the shadows. At first glance it might look like she's being held captive. At second glance, she's pretty clearly armed herself. He's counting on Kasey Aherne being the kind of guy who doesn't delve much beneath the surface.

"You really think he'll fall for it?"

Marta's voice echoes faintly in the silence, and Raj turns from his examination of the warehouse to face her.

"I spent the last month surveilling your grandson," Raj says. "I might not know him as well as you do, but I know Sara Mugisha's got him spooked. If he had proper time to look into his captains' deaths, he'd realize she doesn't have anything to do with that. But he's running scared. The message we faked from Mugisha claiming she's holding you hostage will get him here to talk. Then it's up to you."

"Tell me about Mugisha," Marta says.

"She runs party drugs, booze. Protection for the service industry and sex workers' unions — that sort of thing."

"And my grandson owes her a lot of money."

"Correct. He, ah . . ." Raj realizes he's trying for delicate, but he just saw Marta torture a would-be assassin. She's not the kind of person who needs news broken to her gently. "Basically anything she's got for sale, he's gotten himself hooked on it."

"That fucking idiot."

Raj glances down at her, trying to make out the sweet old tourist woman he'd thought he was meeting at the terminal. Marta's mouth has a hard line to it; her papery hands are folded neatly in front of her, her pistol obscured by the bell sleeve of her new blue jacket. Still, when she glances up at him, her eyes hold a touch of humor, like they're in on a joke together.

He's not sure what joke they're in on, though. He's not quite her bodyguard anymore, now that he's started offering suggestions and she's started taking them. He's not a partner, either. A warm eddy of anticipation surges through him — whatever happens after this, his life doesn't need to be a binary choice between letting himself be trapped in his father's plans or letting the sea take him.

There's a third option. An unknown road. Taking it is terrifying as hell, but at least it'll be his choice.

"I should have come back and made things right after my son died," Marta says. "Instead of letting Kasey make a fool of the Aherne name."

"What happened to letting children and grandchildren take their own path?" Raj asks.

Marta's glance is sharp, but there's an amused twist to her lips that says she doesn't mind having her own words lobbed back at her. Not by him, anyway. Or at least not this time.

"It's every entrepreneur's dream to build a strong business that can continue to support their children," Marta says. "I retired in my prime to give my son a chance to prove himself, and to enjoy the fruit of what I'd built. My grandson, however, couldn't wait for the business to become his. I heard rumors that he helped his father along to an early grave. A few years later, I stopped receiving the dividends I was due — so either the business was in trouble, or my grandson had lost sight of what made him successful."

"So you came back to set things straight."

Marta gives Raj a long look. "I could probably have saved a lot of trouble today if I had just asked if you knew my grandson."

"I think we both could've saved a lot of trouble by asking questions earlier."

Marta's eyes twinkle — and there's the sweet tourist he'd picked up. "Come now," she says. "You've had fun."

"It's been an interesting day."

Raj senses more than hears a change in the dock noise outside the warehouse doors. Voices gathering, orders being given. He straightens and settles a hand on Marta's shoulder. She shivers at the touch — electricity crawls over his skin, too.

"You know," she says. "I like you. If this works, I'm going to need people I can trust to help me get things back on course."

Raj hasn't kept the surprise off his face; Marta smiles faintly, then turns back to the door. His mind probes gently, uncertainly, at the idea of working for Marta Aherne. Fortunately he doesn't need to respond now, because Kasey Aherne throws open the doors.

Even in the weeks since Raj and Ruby finished their surveillance on him, he's grown thinner, more antsy. His movements are jerky and unnatural, like he's either coming down from a high or working up to it. Raj wonders if he was already flying when he got the "meet us here or your grandmother is dead" note, or if he popped a pill to help him deal with the situation.

Maybe the former, because despite the note's warning to come unarmed, he's brought no small amount of fire-power. Either he didn't read it carefully or he doesn't really care if his grandmother gets killed by his blunder. A flare of indignation at Marta's expense blooms in Raj's chest. What kind of monster doesn't care what happens to his own granny?

Kasey Aherne seems completely unconcerned, suit jacket open to reveal his shoulder holster, flanked by almost a dozen of his soldiers. Each of them are armed to the teeth, too, and each one of them is aiming their fury directly at Raj.

The goal is Marta being able to talk them out of this; bar that, he's counting on her assertion that quite a few of Kasey's soldiers are still loyal to her. Raj and Marta are both armed, and Jirayu's waiting somewhere in the wings with his bag of tricks. But the odds here are pretty terrible if it should come to a physical altercation.

A trickle of sweat tingles down Raj's spine; he ignores it, staying loose and ready for whatever comes. Conversation and violence aren't the only tricks up his sleeve right now, just the most reliable. He keeps his hand glued to Marta's shoulder, praying this works.

"What is this?" Kasey growls to Raj as his soldiers fill in behind him. He's stopped just outside the circle of light; they'll need to draw him closer.

"It's nice to see you, too, Kasey," Marta says.

Kasey blinks his attention from Raj to Marta and back. "Where's Mugisha, then?"

"I'm glad you could come," Marta says. "I trust you got my messages this morning."

Kasey frowns at her, balance thrown off by the fact that she's not acting like a hostage. "What are you talking about? I didn't know you were in town." Either he's a terrible liar, or he's not expecting his grandmother to leave this warehouse. "Why didn't you tell me you were coming to visit?"

"I'm not here for a visit," Marta says. "I'm back for good."

Raj has been studying Kasey's soldiers to suss out which will break for Marta if diplomacy shatters; Marta's statement nets him some useful reactions. The woman with the black braids at Kasey's side straightens, her weapon lowering slightly. A man in a white blazer trades his scowl for a look Raj might read as hopeful. The pair watching the door lean in to whisper; one casts an unabashed glare at Kasey's back.

"You're working with Mugisha?" Kasey asks his grandmother.

"Of course not."

Kasey points a finger at Raj. "That man works for her," he says, and Raj winces — apparently Ruby wasn't able to cover their tracks after all. "He's one of her goddamned spies, isn't he."

"Wrong," snaps Marta. Kasey's spine straightens involuntarily at the rebuke. "He was working for me to get information on you. I kept hearing how bad things had gotten here, and I needed to know for myself before I came to set you straight."

"But Mugisha — "

"Kasey Ami Aherne, you'll listen to me." Marta's tone sharpens, and Kasey glances at his people; Raj wonders if he's beginning to regret bringing them here to witness the vicious dressing down. A faint dark flush is creeping into his cheeks, and Raj doesn't get the sense Kasey's the kind of man who takes humiliation well. Kasey shifts his stance uncomfortably, stepping closer to the circle of light, but not close enough.

"You've surrounded yourself with some questionable influences," Marta continues. "I removed them. And I'm back to replace you as head of the business."

"You never let me run it my way to begin with," Kasey snarls. "Always asking for more and more tribute? You say you left me the family business, but you're siphoning off all the profits."

"The increase in amount is called *interest due*, child,"

Marta says impatiently. "And my dividend wouldn't have been a burden if you'd run this business with any sort of sense. When I was in charge, I certainly wasn't dissolving all our profits under my tongue for a cheap high."

People shift at that — Marta's hit a nerve, and Raj marks which soldiers shoot Kasey angry looks. Braids angles her body away from Kasey almost unconsciously. Blazer taps his palm against his thigh. The pair at the door have abandoned their post, coming forward as though to help cover Marta.

Kasey steps forward, toes nudging into the circle of light, face contorted in rage. One more step is all Raj needs out of him; he squeezes Marta's shoulder to remind her, and that spark of electricity slithers over his skin once more. She lifts her chin.

"All that could be forgiven," she says. "But I'll never forgive you for killing your father."

Kasey Aherne roars back with anger — back out of the light — and aims his pistol between his grandmother's eyes. Guns snap to attention around him — but more than Raj was hoping for are trained on him and Marta. The flicker of hope in his gut sinks like a stone.

"You should have died years ago," Kasey snarls, and squeezes the trigger.

12

Lasadi

"**D**on't I know you?"

Eyebrows says it with curiosity more than accusation. He squints at Lasadi, trying to place her, and Lasadi can all but see him sifting through a file of stills in his head.

Lasadi shifts her weight, ready and easy on her feet despite the fact that she probably weighs in at half this man's size. Not to mention his companion, Rockstar — he's no small thing either. She and Jay have the element of surprise until those pieces click into place, but Lasadi doesn't want to go down that path unless she has to. One of the tanks could send out the alarm before they're neutralized, and then this job really will be dead in the black.

Jay catches her eye; she shakes her head as subtly as she can.

"I'd hope you know me," Lasadi says to Eyebrows. "I've been working here the past five years, haven't I, so I've definitely seen you. Now," she says cheerfully, "let's hope we caught this recycler in time, or your boss is going to come home to a surprise."

Eyebrows's scowl deepens, but he seems placated — for now. Rockstar looks mildly alarmed, probably at the prospect of getting anything too nasty on his impeccable shoes.

Jay makes a clicking noise with his tongue: *Bad news.* "Looks like it's backing up on the third floor," he says. He's holding the tablet angled away from Eyebrows and Rockstar, but from her perch on the stairs Las can see the screen. He's managed to sync with the townhouse's security system and is initiating a complete reboot. He shakes his head, eyes widening in faux horror. "It's — oh, shit. Safeguard broke."

"See what you did!" Lasadi tells Eyebrows. "These systems are so shoddy. If they're not gonna spring for a better waste recycler for this wing, at least they could give us a raise. I got an engineering degree, not a 'vacuum shit out of people's carpets' degree." She turns to Jay. "How bad is it? Hazmat suit bad?" When he nods sadly, Lasadi sighs and rummages through the maintenance cart for a pair of emergency film suits. "Don't know if we've got any your size," she says to Eyebrows and Rockstar. "But you're welcome to come with."

Rockstar shakes his head so fast his earrings tangle in his hair. "That's all you, then."

"Fine." Lasadi jerks her head at Jay; the tablet in his hands has just flashed green, thank the olds. "Grab some of those towels and let's head up."

She climbs every step with fear pricking the place between her shoulder blades; Rockstar has been too turned off by the picture she painted of the mess upstairs to think about anything else, but Eyebrows's memory-recall gears are still turning. Slow, but they're turning. They don't have much time to pull the rest of their plan off.

"Did your program work?" she mutters to Jay as they climb the stairs.

"Full system reboot," he says quietly, consulting the floor plan on his tablet. "Should factory-reset all the locks. And Aherne's office is . . . there." He jerks his chin at the door at the end of the hallway. The door has a bulky biolock, but right now it's flashing green with the message AWAITING SERVICE RESET.

"Let's see where Kasey Aherne runs his empire," she says, pushing the door open.

The office is a dump. Chairs and cushions pushed to the edges of the room, the desk shoved back to make room for what looks like a top-notch projector. An abstract holosense play is pulsing through the middle of the room and a skull wreath abandoned on one of the chairs still blinks with light. The viewer — probably Aherne — tore it off without bothering to stop the show.

The desk is cracked, with traces of what looks like the best Indiran snow money can buy caught in the spider-webbed glass. There's a tumble of neon-pink pills spilled out on one shelf, and the fabrics of the room reek from cigar smoke and stale sweat.

"Less running his empire, more running high," Jay says.

"No wonder he stole from Nico," Lasadi says. "Didn't have two brain cells left to tell him what a bad idea it was." She scans the room, looking for a sign of Aherne's safe. "You head to the recycler in case one of those two tanks come up here. I'll — "

"Wait," booms a voice behind them. Lasadi spins,

blinking against the throbbing lights of the holosense play. The gears behind Eyebrows's skull have finally clicked into place and he's looming in the doorway to the stairs. "I know why I know you."

"I told you," Lasadi says impatiently, shifting in front of Jay. She turns back to Eyebrows, holding one hand behind her back, palm up, and feels the reassuring grip of the pistol Jay sets there. "I've worked here for five years."

"You were at Campeche! You killed Niñerola."

He charges with a roar. Lasadi flicks the safety off with her thumb, gets off one shot — it buries itself in Eyebrows's shoulder but doesn't stop his mass. He tackles her and she lands against the arm of a couch with a grunt, the pistol thrown free from her grip. She ducks one meaty fist — it splinters the wall, showering her with composite — then drives a knee between his legs.

Eyebrows goes rigid with pain. She shoves him and he tips back, stumbling through the blinding, writhing colors of the holoplay, blood streaming black down one arm, good hand groping for a weapon.

Lasadi rolls as he swings a side table at her, scattering Indiran snow like rainbow glitter through the holoplay. Something stabs painful in her hip; she ignores it and ducks as the side table flies by her. It crashes through the window, leaving a jagged maw in the floor-to-ceiling glass.

The glaring light from outside the dark room paints Eyebrows's face in a mask of rage. He lunges for Lasadi, but she's faster. She feints left, leaps right, landing on the back of the couch with a grunt. She aims a roundhouse kick at his back; her boot connects with solid muscle.

It doesn't seem to faze Eyebrows, but it does keep him stumbling forward. He's lost his footing in the litter of broken glass and crumbled wall composite and Indiran snow, and lost his sight to the wildly flickering holoplay. When he reaches for something to stop his momentum, his hand finds only the jagged edge of the broken window.

And then there's nothing but an Eyebrows-shaped hole in what was left of the glass.

Lasadi slides down the back of the couch, but doesn't let herself sit even though her legs feel like they're made of impact gel. The projector got shattered at some point during the fight and the room is bathed in blissful calm — but Jay's not here, and somewhere in the back of her mind during the fight she registered gunshots coming from the hall.

"Jay!" she yells, scooping her pistol from where it fell and taking cover beside the door. She's just about to swing out when Jay answers.

"All clear," he says. Lasadi lowers her gun, exits the office. Jay's standing at the top of the stairs, a stun carbine slung over one shoulder. She follows his gaze to find Rockstar in a tangle of unmoving limbs at the bottom.

Jay slips his pistol into the pocket of his mechanic overalls and yawns his jaw, rubbing at a sore spot. He doesn't seem to be bleeding anywhere.

"You good?" she asks.

"I'm very over this job."

"Me, too," Las says. "Let's grab what we came for and get out of here."

13

Raj

The room explodes in a concussive array of rainbow sparks, and Raj can't tell if they're real or just his skull lighting up behind his squeezed-shut eyes. A light above them shatters, raining down shards of glass, but his skin is singing with electricity and he barely feels it.

He dives for Marta before Kasey can get another shot off, mildly stunned that they're both still alive.

Vash's experimental exploding shield is terrifying, but it works. The tiny part of his mind that isn't preoccupied with survival is cataloguing his feedback: wearing it makes your skin crawl, and it sucks all the air out of your lungs when it detonates. The thick reek of scorched skin and blood clogs his nostrils — he hopes that's an aftereffect and not a sign that he or Marta are injured.

Oh. And the explosion didn't extend far enough to hit Kasey Aherne.

Kasey's second shot thuds into Raj's chest armor when Raj dives in front of Marta, a combination of the explosion and Kasey's drug twitches ruining his aim. Raj grunts at the impact — he's wearing high-end stuff left over from his Arquellian navy days, but Kasey was close.

He lets their momentum roll him and Marta behind a crate; she pushes herself into a crouch and squeezes off a pair of shots. The big man with the reddish beard — the one who was charging at their hiding spot — goes down with blood blooming on his chest.

Grandma's still got it.

"Who do I shoot?" Raj yells to Marta. His voice sounds underwater, thick; that the experimental exploding shield fucks with your hearing is another piece of feedback for Vash.

"Just cover me," she yells back.

Kasey's team is in chaos. Braids is wrestling him for his gun, but she doesn't seem to be trying to hurt him. "That's your fucking *grandmother*," she yells as another of Kasey's men grabs her from behind. She breaks his grip and spins, punching him in the jaw, then turns to face her next attacker, a tall man with spiked purple hair. Raj's shot takes Spikes through the neck without waiting for confirmation from Marta.

"That one was good, right?" Raj asks. Marta nods and fires at a tattooed woman who's been taking potshots at them from the other side of the warehouse.

The man in the white blazer has taken out a couple more of Kasey's loyal soldiers, and soon Braids and Blazer are fighting back-to-back near the pile of crates Marta and Raj took shelter behind. They're joined by the couple who were standing back by the door — but Raj doesn't have time to dissect the shifting loyalties of the Aherne organization at the moment because Kasey himself is leaping over the pile of crates to get to them.

Raj catches him midair, angles his body so that when

they hit the ground rolling, Kasey acts as his cushion. The impact still slams through his bones — he's going to need more than a nice hot shower to ease today's bruises.

Start the day putting on your nicest suit to trail a tourist around the Bell, end it by wrestling on the floor with one of Artemis City's major crime lords. Story of his life, Raj might have said earlier today, complete with a self-deprecating laugh. Only now he can see exactly what Ruby means. She's not willing to roll the dice on her day — she wants to know what they're getting into so she can be prepared. So she can come home each day to her brother.

Raj is starting to see the appeal.

He ducks Kasey's wild swing and sends Ruby a silent thought of apology. If he makes it out of this, he'll have a few people to do right by.

Kasey Aherne is a scrappy, vicious fighter. Raj clearly has more hand-to-hand combat training, but Kasey makes up for it with his fury — and whatever drug is currently spiking his bloodstream. The other man swipes at Raj with clawed fingers, teeth bared and snarling. Raj twists out of the way, elbow to Kasey's gut, and breaks the grip, rocking back up to a crouch. He dodges as Kasey lunges at him, yelps when Kasey's heel connects with his shin. The leg still bears weight, so Raj plants his feet and grips Kasey by the shoulders, using the momentum of the man's next swing to fling him past and send him crashing into another stack of crates.

The top one crashes down, the hasp shattering and spools of industrial electrical insulation spilling out over the floor of the warehouse.

"Fight's over," he calls to Kasey, who's peeling himself off the ground, teeth bloody, panting for breath. Raj spots his pistol where it landed near the table, scoops it from the floor, and covers Kasey, keeping his body in between the snarling madman and Marta.

"No one wants to hurt you," Marta calls. "We're just here to help."

The fury of the fight is ebbing around them, and as far as Raj can tell, Marta's loyalists have won. A few of Kasey's people are restrained, a few are lying prone on the bloody ground — precision shots through the eye suggest Jirayu. But the rest have either given up their weapons or decided to join Braids and Blazer.

Braids steps forward, making herself the de facto spokesperson of the loyalist Aherne faction. "It's good to have you back, ma'am," she says.

Marta holds her arms wide, pulling Braids in for a brief hug. "It's good to be back." She smiles at the others. "I don't recommend retirement," she says.

Blazer grins back. "I always said retirement wouldn't suit you, ma'am."

Marta turns back to her grandson. "Now. As for you — "

Kasey screams and lunges for her.

Raj aims to wound — Kasey may be taking aim at Raj's client, but he's still not sure how Marta would take to him killing her grandson — but when Kasey hits the ground his eyes have rolled back in his head.

Panic grips Raj until he spots the tranq dart in Kasey's neck along with the bullet hole Raj put in his arm.

Jirayu.

As if summoned, Marta's driver-slash-assassin-slash-who-knows-what appears from the shadows, rifle slung over his shoulder. Braids's eyes widen when she sees him, then she grins in greeting. Jirayu lifts his chin, a smile on his lips.

Marta straightens, like a queen among her people. "Tell everyone Marta Aherne is out of retirement," she says. She looks down her nose at her grandson, then motions for two of her new soldiers to grab him. "Let's get him back home," she says. "It's time he and I had a heart-to-heart."

Raj doesn't seem to be included in the barrage of orders Marta's barking at her crew, so he props a hip on the corner of the table and loosens the straps of his body armor, probing gently at the spot where he took a bullet for her. Nothing's broken, but he'll have a hell of a bruise over the next few weeks — a good reminder of how this day could have ended.

This morning maybe he would have said drowning in a blaze of glory in an Artemisian warehouse was a fitting end to the short and turbulent chronicles of Raj Demetriou. Now, though, something else is tugging at his subconscious. Like the quiet, certain knowledge that the dark smudge on the horizon is land after days of floating adrift in the sea.

He pushes himself off the table and holsters his pistol. Buttons his suit jacket — which is now ruined beyond repair — with a wince. What's left of Kasey Aherne's little crew is now leaping to do Marta's bidding. Blazer's directing the cleanup of the warehouse, while Braids and Jirayu have exchanged bear hugs and are in position on either side of Marta as guards.

Looks like Raj's job as day bodyguard to Sweet Grandma Marta is finished, which is just fine by him.

She meets his gaze across the room as he approaches,

amusement twisting her lips into a smile. She waves off Jirayu and Braids.

"I had a lovely day, thank you," Marta says.

"You're welcome, ma'am."

"Although your friend's . . . experiment could use some refinement." She rubs her arms with a tiny shiver. "I still feel like ants are crawling over my skin."

"It worked, though."

Marta laughs. "It did. Tell her she has a buyer if she can work out the kinks."

"I'll pass that on." Though Raj can't imagine Vash agreeing to deal with a Pearls crime lord; it's not her style.

Marta tilts her head, studying him. "I don't suppose you're looking for a full-time position? It's hard to find someone who's skilled at both protection and conversation."

Raj takes a deep breath.

Somewhere out on the horizon, that dark smudge is wavering, ready to vanish forever if Raj doesn't keep his gaze locked on it and swim that direction as hard as he possibly can. Marta's offering him stability, at least for the moment. But it's a siren's call compared to what he actually needs.

"Thank you, ma'am, but I don't think that's for me."

"I understand. But don't be a stranger." She pats his arm. "I've had Jirayu send the funds for today, it should be in your account."

Raj smiles and bows his head to Marta. Shakes hands with Jirayu and Braids, then lets himself out. At first he's not sure where he's headed — just, away from the complications in the shattered warehouse — but he finds himself taking the lift down from the warehousing sector to the Bell's glass observation ring.

He remembers the first time he stepped out into this view. He'd been staying with a friend in Ironfall when he first washed up in the Pearls, and had agreed to do a few day's work in Artemis City. Ironfall is closed in, compact — it's easy enough to imagine you're on a large spaceship, which Raj was familiar with from the navy. But Artemis City's open Bell drives home the unfamiliarity of life in Durga's Belt: *You've never been anywhere like this before.*

He strolls the observation ring comfortably, now, dodging tourists who are staring through the glass below their feet at the lattice of plazas and bridges and zipping transports, deep into the glittering neon heart of the city. Others crane their necks to look up through the glass dome that tops the Bell to where ships are maneuvering in and out of the dockyard ring. Raj can't see the stars beyond, but he knows they're there. Artemis City's observation ring is meant to make you feel that a whole world has opened up to you, but the vastness of space is full of possibilities beyond.

He's not trapped here, he realizes. Not in Artemis City, not even in the Pearls. He may have come here to hide; that doesn't mean he has to die here in exile.

Raj pulls out his comm and swipes open the message he'd received from Vash this morning. He can't help the smile that tugs at his lips when her face fills the screen at an awkward angle.

"Raj! It's been too long. Hope you're keeping out of trouble. Listen, Gracie and I have a little thing you could help us with, maybe. A rare item in a private collection in Artemis City. Let me know if you're interested. Either way, come by, we'd love to see you. Stay well."

The comm lurches nauseatingly as she cuts the

connection, and he opens the attachment she sent. He scans the history lesson Gracie wrote up about the object to get the basics — thought to be some ritualistic artifact from a Tisare settlement on a remote asteroid — then studies the image itself. An obsidian scepter the length of his forearm, carved with the motif of a strange, stylized bird, wings stretched overhead, spiraling upwards.

Vash has attached information on the mark, too, an Artemisian tech giant and private collector named Parr Sumilang, who just happens to be throwing a big party tomorrow night.

The way gigs for Vash and Gracie usually go is this: He works a big job for someone else so he can scrape together the resources to fetch their trinket or shipment of rare supplies or whatever it is they need this month, charters a ship to deliver it to their station, and spends a week on their quirky rock enjoying the only peace he's had in the last three years and telling himself he's going to leave any day now.

He's been letting jobs for Vash and Gracie get further and further between — not only because he hasn't been able to afford to take them on, but because it's been getting harder and harder to leave their home every time he walks in.

This morning, he might have deleted Vash's message unread and told himself she was better off for it.

Now, though? He may not know much, but he knows that dark smudge of shore on the horizon seems more solid when he thinks about taking this job.

He opens up a response, recording video on the off chance Gracie actually watches it.

"Hey, Vash. Good to hear from you. I'm game — I'll do some recon and let you know if I need any more information. And by the way, I just had a chance to use your exploding shield. Long story — can't wait to tell you all about it. Give my love to Gracie."

He leans elbows against the railing and flips back to the image, tracing a finger over it. He has until tomorrow night to come up with a plan — a well-baked plan — to get himself into a party and walk out with this artifact. Plenty of time to make sure he gets things right.

He calls up the profile of the tech giant who's throwing the party and begins to plan. Around him, tourists eddy through the ring, the lights of Artemis City glittering in their wide eyes, each one looking for their own path home.

14

Lasadi

There's nothing like that first breath Lasadi takes every time she enters the *Nanshe*. It's like breathing helium, inhaling a deep buoyancy that does more than lift her mood. It lifts her body — makes her steps lighter, her shoulders straighter, her joints freer. Even the taut and aching burn scars over her ribs and thigh seem to release, letting her walk more free as soon as the bay doors to the *Nanshe* seal and lock behind her and Jay.

"I've never been so glad to be home," she says.

The *Nanshe*'s a Mapalad Lowboy cargo hauler, designed for the trade routes of Durga's Belt but more than suited for longer-haul trips to the inner planets or Bixia Yuanjin if need be. Lowboys are known for their storage capacity more than their good looks, but Nico Garnet had upgraded the *Nanshe* a fair amount even before Lasadi and Jay got hold of her. Now the *Nanshe* is surprisingly nimble and quick, a pure joy to fly.

It's got a pair of shuttles, a spacious cargo hold, ingenious caches for contraband, and a relatively comfortable crew deck with a galley meant for gathering. Jay likes to remind her the *Nanshe* can crew six with room to spare, but Lasadi has gotten used to the solitude. And walking into this ship to find silence except for the familiar faint hum of the standby systems? No tool out of place? Nothing in the air but the scent of the grease Jay uses in the engine? That's priceless.

This ship is her haven — and it won't be Nico's for much longer. Just a few paydays more.

Jay's giving her a strange look.

"What?"

"Home?" He shrugs. "I haven't heard you say that about anywhere. Not since."

He doesn't say since when, and he doesn't have to. Since the war ended and they lost the chance to stay in the home they'd been fighting for.

Lasadi waves a hand, skin pricking between her shoulder blades; she hadn't realized she'd said it out loud. "You know. A place to relax. Where you don't have to watch your back."

Jay shrugs. "Sounds like home to me." He drops his own duffel beside hers, like always. "I'm just glad to hear you say it. Personally, I'll feel better once we're back in Ironfall."

Lasadi ignores that sharp little blade under her ribs. Of course he wants to get back to Ironfall, to Chiara, to his own apartment. Lasadi could have her own apartment in Ironfall, too — Nico has offered a place in his compound, or, she has enough income to afford something of her own, like Jay. She stays on the *Nanshe* because she's saving money, she'd say, but it's more than that.

This is where she feels most comfortable. This is her own place, where she can move on her own power. This is what freedom feels like. Maybe it's lonely at times — and about to become lonelier once Jay decides he's done with her. But at least it'll still be hers.

She pushes all that aside.

"You can't tell me that wasn't a little bit fun," she says, making for the ladder to the crew deck.

"I think we have different definitions of fun," Jay calls after her.

"Adventure? Twists that keep you on your toes?"

"Getting shot at by gangsters or almost arrested for murder?"

She spins herself onto the ladder and grins at him. Jay's trying to look serious, but that dimple betrays him. "Yeah," Lasadi says. "Fun."

Jay finally gives in with a laugh. "Fine. I had some good times today. But I have a demand for next time."

Her heart soars at the simple words: *next time.* "Whatever you want."

"If you want hackery shit done, we hire a hacker." He folds his well-toned arms over his chest, fixing her with a look.

"Okay," she says. "Next job that needs a hacker, we'll hire one for real."

"And maybe some more muscle." Jay lifts an eyebrow. "Don't look at me like that. We'll vet them careful, and we'll make sure they're a good fit. It won't change a thing."

It'll change everything. But Lasadi pushes aside visions of strangers invading her space. "I need to go check in with Nico," she says.

"I'll get us prepped for launch," he says. "After I shower. Order us some takeout, yeah?"

He disappears through the door to his cabin as Lasadi climbs up to the crew deck. There are four cabins on this level, but Jay stays on the cargo level to be close to the engines; Lasadi's cabin — the only door open in the hall — is closest to the hatch to the bridge. She palms the hatch open and settles into her pilot's chair, again glancing around to see that nothing's out of place. It's easy to do, she doesn't leave many personal items out.

She calls up a live connection to Nico — the delay between the Pearl's dwarf planets is minimal enough for that — and is surprised when Nico's daughter answers.

"Lasadi," Tora says. She's as polished and professional as always, though with that increasingly noticeable tinge of worry in the press of her lips. "Good to hear from you. Were you successful?"

"We were," Las replies. "We're getting ready to head back your way."

"Hold off on that." Tora leans in to her screen as though typing something; Lasadi waits to speak, not wanting to talk over Tora in the lag. Tora straightens. "Another job has come up — this one will take you to Auburn Station — and there's something you'll need to retrieve from Artemis City first."

Lasadi's eyes widen. "Auburn Station?"

"You've heard of it," Tora says, her tone wry.

Everyone's heard of Auburn Station. Ghost pirates, bloodthirsty raiders, deadly curses, straight-up demonic evil? It's a good story for belt drifters to tell after they've thrown back a few beers.

"I thought it was demolished years ago," Lasadi says carefully.

"I'll brief you on the job when you get back to Ironfall," Tora says; Lasadi notes the *I'll*. Combine that with the fact that Tora answered this line, Nico must be getting sicker. "I just sent information about the item we need you to pick up."

The *Nanshe*'s control panel pings, and Lasadi swipes open the attachment. "Got it."

"The Auburn Station job is bigger than you and Jay," Tora says. "We can vet some additional crew when you return."

Lasadi doesn't think she's reacted, but Tora sighs sharply.

"That's not negotiable, so pick some people you think you can work with. I'll see you soon."

Tora's cut the connection before Lasadi can reply, and Lasadi resists the urge to make a rude gesture towards the place where Tora's hologram just sat. At least it sounds like Tora's giving her leeway in who she chooses. Jay must have some friends who would fit the bill and won't get in her way.

Except.

A flush of realization washes through her. In all the crush of their success, coming home, getting the new job from Tora, she'd completely ignored what Jay'd said in the safehouse.

"I think I'm done working for Nico," he'd said. "I *think*."

She takes a deep breath and hits the intercom. "Jay?" She waits a moment, but he doesn't answer — of course, he's in the shower. An operations panel on the dashboard confirms that the water's flowing in the cargo-level bath.

Let him get clean and relaxed and she can soften the news with dinner. Since they're not going to eat and run back to Ironfall, they can go out. She'll splurge for his favorite curry spot by the terminal.

Lasadi opens the attachment Tora sent, then leans in to study the holographic diagram with surprise.

It's not the usual, not the black market goods or strange weapons tech Nico deals in — at least not on the outside. The object is a black stick, intricately carved with a winged figure that spirals up the shaft. It's some sort of totem, the description says, held in the private collection of a local tech giant. Tora's left a note in the file that the mark is having some sort of party tomorrow night, which would be a good opportunity to get close.

Lasadi sets the hologram spinning on her dashboard with the swipe of a finger, intrigued despite herself.

"One last job for Nico," she murmurs, even though Jay can't hear her. "Then you and I are home free."

Welcome to the Nanshe Chronicles

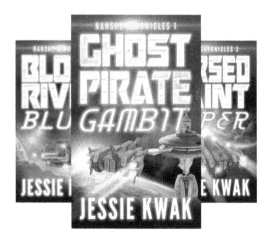

The adventure continues in *Ghost Pirate Gambit*.

Get it at jessiekwak.com

About Jessie Kwak

Jessie Kwak has always lived in imaginary lands, from Arrakis and Ankh-Morpork to Earthsea, Tatooine, and now Portland, Oregon. As a writer, she sends readers on their own journeys to immersive worlds filled with fascinating characters, gunfights, explosions, and dinner parties.

When she's not raving about her latest favorite sci-fi series to her friends, she can be found sewing, mountain biking, or out exploring new worlds both at home and abroad.

Author photo by Robert Kittilson.

Connect with me:
www.jessiekwak.com
jessie@jessiekwak.com

The Bulari Saga

**With stakes this high, humanity doesn't need a
hero. They need someone who can win.**

**Complete 5-book series + 3 prequel novellas + bonus short
stories = over 500,000 words of adventure.**

Willem Jaantzen didn't ask to be a hero. He just wants to keep
his family safe in the shifting sands of Bulari's underground—
and to get the city's upper crust to acknowledge just how far
he's come since his days as an orphaned street kid. With his
businesses thriving and his dark past swept into the annals of
history, it looks like he has everything he could ever ask for.

Until, that is, his oldest rival turns up murdered and the blame —and champagne—begins to flow.

It turns out Thala Coeur died as she lived: sowing chaos. And when a mysterious package bearing her call sign shows up on Jaantzen's doorstep, he and his family are quickly swallowed up in a web of lies, betrayals, and interplanetary politics. It'll only take one stray spark to start another civil war in the underworld, and Jaantzen's going to have to pull out every play from his notorious past if he wants to keep his city from going up in flames.

Jaantzen never wanted to be a hero, but that might just be a good thing. Because a hero could never stop the trouble that's heading humanity's way.

The Bulari Saga is a five-book series featuring gunfights, dinner parties, explosions, motorcycle chases, underworld intrigue, and a fiercely plucky found family who have each other's backs at every step. Perfect for fans of The Expanse, Firefly, and The Godfather.

Start the adventure today at www. jessiekwak.com/bulari-saga

Did you like the book?

As a reader, I rely on book recommendations to help me pick what to read next.

As a writer, book recommendations are the most powerful way for me to get the word out to new readers.

If you liked this book, please tell a friend! It's the easiest way to help authors you enjoy keep producing great work.

Cheers!

Jessie